# Family Man

Best wishes to Wide,

Annabel Alderman

# Family Man

A Novel

By

Annabel Alderman

MERCER UNIVERSITY PRESS
1979        1999
TWENTY YEARS OF PUBLISHING EXCELLENCE

ISBN 0-86554-646-0
MUP/H482

First Edition.

∞The paper used in this publication meets the minimum requirements of American National Standard for Information Sciences — Permanence of Paper for Printed Library Materials, ANSI Z39.48-1984.

*Library of Congress Cataloging-in-Publication Data*

# Acknowledgments

Whatever has been my determined pursuit, help has always come from unexpected sources and in all manner of disguises. I have come to view that dependable phenomenon as God-sponsored synchronicity, sweeping me along in some unseen pattern of "doing."

So went the writing of this novel, and the subsequent, timely appearance of the variegated brigade that pressed *Family Man* toward its publication. For all those who made available the crucial assistance, in whatever mode and at whatever perfect moment, I am forever grateful.

To single out but a few:

My long-time friend, Atlanta attorney Marc Davis, first to read the raw manuscript, first to embolden my novelist ambitions;

Bill Emerson, genial man of letters whose significant literary legacy reaches across several decades, who fanned the smoldering flame;

Pat Watters, newspaperman in the grand tradition, whose several book chronicles of our turbulent Sixties and Seventies are lasting literary gems, who, along with his witty, wise and one-of-a-kind wife, Glenda, did not laugh and point when I declared my intent to become a novelist;

Roy Reed, having done a noble stint with *The New York Times* and thereafter having finely crafted the definitive biography of Orval Faubus, who endorsed my novel-writing fervor;

Matt Flumerfelt, Mary Freelove, Marjorie Doughty, Mavis Harrell, Ann Harris, Rodney Hull, and Bailey Mapp, all of the *South Georgia Writers Guild*, who inspired, critiqued and cheered me on;

Mary Hood, renowned creator of rare and wonderful fiction, who graciously invited me to Berry College to read, before an array of literary luminaries and talented aspirants, from my yet unpublished, alleged novel;

Cleon "Bro" Knight, dear, enduring friend and fellow political-watcher, who encouraged, badgered, consoled, chauffeured, ran errands, escorted me to Waffle House lunches, swept my carport and read the 'script, never failing to counsel strength of purpose;

Stanley Booth, blues music historian and, consequently, my soul brother (his latest work, *Dance With the Devil,* is an erudite recounting of the story of the Rolling Stones), who rode to the rescue during the final days of editing;

Galen Mirate, beloved daughter and my experienced roadie from earlier days, masquerading as my technological consultant, whose unstinting attention to detail converted my haphazard paper blizzard into acceptable manuscript form;

Eugene Patterson, Editor Emeritus of *The St. Petersburg (FL) Times,* to whom this book is dedicated, and by whose deft hand, alone, *Family Man* was elevated to publishable status, and

Marc Jolley, assistant publisher of Mercer University Press, who blithely took on the task of editing this manuscript, and whose unending, gentle patience with my novice-based foibles has sustained me through many a re-write. In so doing, he has carved his name upon my heart.

Annabel Alderman
26 February 1999

*For Eugene Patterson*

# 1

## "Answer Th' Phone When It Rings, Darlin' "

*ON THE ROAD AGAIN*

Wheeler Boone had been thinking about moving his family to Wyoming ever since he headed west from south Georgia four days earlier. Driving out of here would be different, but he could handle it. He took pride in knowing what it took to be a first class road warrior, and in knowing he had it.

After seven years of hauling produce out of Pensacola and five more of rumbling across the country hauling steel girders out of Jacksonville, he was more than ready for a change. He knew Myra might not like the cold country, but she wasn't a woman to argue after the man of the family had made a decision.

Coming out of the truck stop cafe that Monday morning at dawn, he warmed to the notion of living right there in Cheyenne. It was a long way from Lolacolola County, Georgia. Besides being in a completely new part of the world, he would be loose from his problem in Lake City, Florida. If money could solve Sandy Whatley's problem, he could always dip into the secret stash he kept under the seat of his tractor. Surely, she didn't really believe he was going to give up his kids and Myra for some truck stop floozy.

*She ought to knowed better'n what she done, anyhow,* he decided, *'less she was jus' tryin' to trap me....* Considering his mama and her response to the Sandy thing gave Wheeler a chill. His daddy would be bad enough, but she was the one he dreaded. She'd throw a fit in proportion to her life's work as a woman of the cloth if she ever found out about Sandy, but Wheeler intended that she never would know.

Back in the truck, he was finally underway and bound for Pendleton, Oregon. That treacherous downhill in, and the even worse uphill out, still had the power to make him nervous. One incautious maneuver and he and that Peterbilt would never see home again.

Home had become dearer to him since the trouble with Sandy came up. It seemed that Myra was more valuable, more noticeably nice looking. For a long time before then, he had taken her for granted. Now, her long, black hair in a plait down her back and her black eyes under that high, round forehead provided him some kind of comfort he had not needed before.

Even her angular frame made sense to Wheeler like it never had. Sandy's green-eyed, slightly buxom self had been so different — so unlike anything he'd been accustomed to. A man could go crazy just thinking about Sandy if it weren't for that flaw she'd developed a few months back.

*One thing for damn certain,* he noted to himself, *Myra don't go against nothin' I tell 'er. 'Course, she ain't really pretty like some women — well, not nothin' like Sandy — but she's healthy as a ox, an' don't mind to work. Hell, if she was in Sandy Whatley's place, she wouldn't never even a-mentioned it to me. She'd'a just took care of it on her own. Damn it all t'hell, I thought me an' Sandy had a*

*understandin' that she wouldn't git pregnant. You can't trust nogoddambody no more.*
He had considered calling Myra on the telephone the night before, but something told him it would just scare her if it rang at night. So he'd let it go. She hadn't been enthusiastic about having a telephone in the first place. *I might as well t'left it off if we ain't never gon' use it,* he thought. *I b'lieve I'll just git it took out when I git back.*
The time had been when he'd called Sandy every night. He'd quit that nearly seven months ago, but he still ached sometimes to hear her high, breathless, "Wheeler! Darlin', is that you?"
*That's awright, Miss Priss,* he fantasized to his erstwhile love, Sandy, *they's other women an' other towns an' a helluva lot of phones. I could even tell you about one in Macclenny, right now, that's by God a-waitin' for me t'ring it.*
Wheeler didn't know how Myra sounded on the phone. He'd never called her. Maybe he'd call her tonight. Then again, maybe not.

*MEANWHILE, BACK IN THE WOODS*
Myra poured some more hot water out of the kettle into the dish pan and thrust both chapped hands deep in the water. There weren't many dishes again that night, since nobody ate but her and the children. It was Wednesday and Wheeler was still on the road.
*Pore ol' Wheeler,* she thought, *tryin' to make us a livin' on a big ol' Peterbilt, gone from home so much, haulin' them steel girders all over th' country.*
As far as Myra could tell, he was about as good, steady a man as a woman could want.
Wheeler was tall—about six feet, one—and weighed close to 200 pounds. Another thing, he could tame a semi, if anybody wanted to know.

Myra wondered what he thought about, up and down the roads like that. Did he think about her and their two boy children? Or about his sturdy, raw-boned and righteous mama, Naomi, who had been a charismatic evangelical preacher since before either one of her sons was born? Or about his peg-legged papa, Merrill, with the dairy herd and the lush strips of marijuana plants that bordered his back pastures? Or maybe his brother, Hayden, who was doing time in Reidsville for shooting a trooper?

She'd always liked her brother-in-law, and Wheeler had acted a few times as if something else was going on between his brother and Myra.

*Didn't Wheeler see,* she mused, *that Hayden was just one of them sweet guys that didn't mind helpin' his sister-in-law with th' chores?* She smiled, thinking back to when her boys were babies and Hayden would see about them with as tender a hand as a woman. She thought of the way he would sit on the porch and rock a fretful baby until midnight, if that's what it took to soothe it.

After that, he'd come back in the house, and get a drink or two of his pa's home-made liquor. Then, a lot of times, he'd get in his pickup and head out to party in the wildest honky-tonks he could find south of Macon.

Hayden kept a gun on his person all the time, but nobody ever wanted to try his skill or his patience bad enough to tangle with him. Not till that rookie trooper, who hollered at Hayden, "Drag your low-life, scummy butt outta th' truck, maggot! Put your damn law-breakin' paws on your goddern, rotten, mule-eared jug head! An' don't gimme no goddam redneck backsass!" That was the one Hayden finally had to shoot.

Myra always thought that judge was wrong to sentence Hayden to 40 years, especially since the trooper, who was only shot in the flesh below his thumb, was back on the road in ten days' time. Drawing his weapon on Hayden had been a mistake that the trooper realized, too late, when Hayden's one, defensive shot sent his gun spinning through the air, across the ditch and into the swamp. It was an apologetic Hayden who drove the wounded trooper to the hospital in Harlow and waited while the doctor sewed him up.

Myra went back over that fateful night again, telling herself about it as she had done hundreds of times before: *Hayden had been a-drinkin', an' hadn't nobody said he weren't. But he weren't drivin' crazy, nor nothin' like that — just goin' to th' house after a few dances an' a few drinks of store whiskey in one of them dives. Dooley Mack's baby sister, Florentine, was right there in th' truck with Hayden, an' she ain't never got over it. To this day, she just busts out a-cryin' in church sometimes, an' they have to tote her out.*

In truth, Hayden's route to Reidsville was not too much out of the ordinary. Never having been to court, Hayden did not take the warrant nor the indictment very seriously. He showed up without a lawyer, assuming that he would merely tell the judge what happened and that the trooper would back him up. Both of them knew that Hayden had fired on the officer in order to keep the trooper, in a moment of panic, from shooting him. It seemed simple enough.

Instead, the trooper, by then transferred to Rome, did not appear. At the time, he was hospitalized with a broken leg brought on by a car crash during a high-speed chase with a real criminal. So a perplexed and unwitting Hayden, in earnest compliance with the district attorney's rather pointed suggestion, signed a plea of guilty to felony assault on a police officer. The judge didn't have much of a sentencing choice after that.

Right or wrong, there he was in Reidsville, and Myra was certain that somebody out of the family ought to go see about Hayden, now and then. It usually fell her lot because Wheeler was gone so much; and his mama and papa had such a large farming operation that they couldn't leave for long at a time.

Myra didn't really care what anybody said, she knew her duty. Hayden had a way of making her feel better about his being in prison. You might say he was her comfort, instead of the other way around. Every time she went, he'd hug her when she got there, and then again when she was getting ready to go. A person can never tell why it is that one little thing like that can mean so much.

### IT'S HANDY TO HAVE A PHONE

The telephone was still something new at the house. Wheeler had it put in "in case you need t'call somebody," but she didn't know who she'd call, nor what for. Wheeler's folks had a phone, all right, but she could tell them all she had to tell in person, so she never felt the need to call them.

*I got a bunch of guns in the house in case anybody wants to break in,* Myra reminded herself, *an' a good, four-year-old pickup parked there by the porch in case one of the young'uns gits sick. That phone's just something Wheeler thought we ought to have since everybody else has got one. I ain't never argued with his decisions before; ain't no use startin' about a danged telephone.*

So the Wheeler Boone household had a phone, silent from the hour of installation.

It was nearly ten o'clock and she had finished "wipin' up th' kitchen," as her mama used to say, when "that thing" rang.

*Lordy, who could that be?* Then, *Oh, God, somethin's happened to Wheeler. . .*

Myra ran to the living room and grabbed up the handset. "Hello? Hello?"

"Is this Miz Boone?" asked a female voice on the other end.

"Yeah, yeah, this is her."

"Miz Wheeler Boone? Myra Boone?" persisted the caller.

"Yeah! What is it? This is Miz Boone. This is Myra. Who is this?"

Myra was beginning to panic. She knew something was wrong. Bad wrong.

She rested her gaze on the blue painted wall by the door, and tried to decide if she'd like it better if it was painted some other color—maybe yellow—instead. Her heart began to pound slowly, as if preparing her for the worst, still ahead.

"What is it? Who is this a-callin'?" she heard herself say again. "Who you want to talk to?"

"Uh, Miz Boone—Myra—uh, my name is, uh, Sandra Whatley...uh, Sandy?" It sounded like a question. "An', uh, Myra...uh, I'm callin' you from the Diamond Horseshoe Truck Stop?–it's, like, right close to Lake City?"

*Oh, God, it's Wheeler–I knew it! Lord, I reckon he's dead.*

The woman's voice on the phone went on. More like, stumbled on.

"Uh, Miz Boone? I mean, Myra—uh, I'm kindly in a tight, an' I was wondering..."

"Is somethin' wrong with Wheeler?" Myra didn't care who else had a problem. "Has he had a wreck?"

"Who? Wheeler? He ain't had no wreck, not that I know of. But I ain't exactly callin' you about Wheeler. Well, yeah, I guess it is about him, too."

Myra looked at her right hand there on the door jamb, and wondered why it was shaking so hard. She suddenly felt sick.

"Sandra, did you say? Uh, Sandy? Sandy, who? Whatley? Well, what you want with me?"

Myra heard Sandy's ragged, sighing breath, heard a jangling sound, like a whole armful of bracelets, maybe; and heard a juke box in the background — "...an' I remember to another you're still married, an' I know there must be more to love than this..."

"See, Myra," said Sandy, "I'm, well, like, p.g.? (again, the question, followed by a long pause) an' uh, I'm needin' some help (and another pause)...so I thought, uh, I'd try to get in touch with you an' maybe you could, uh..."

"In touch with me? What for?" A puzzled Myra just couldn't square any part of the conversation.

"Well, uh, because...see, it's Wheeler's."

"Wheeler's? Wheeler's what? What're you talkin' about, woman?"

"It's Wheeler's baby I'm gonna have."

This time, it was a major pause. Myra eased down to a squat on the linoleum, smoothed her apron, and tasted the words, very softly, "Wheeler's baby?"

Sandy had gained some composure in those silent moments, and had found a stronger voice.

"Yes, ma'am. An' it's Wheeler's, all right. 'Cause, see, he's been my one an' only for a good, long time now. I mean, see, he told me y'all was separated, an' we talked about gettin' married an' everything. So, I mean, when I turned up p.g., I just thought maybe then we'd go on an' get married. Then, when I told him, he just said he'd try to think of something. But I haven't seen him in four or five months, an' I'm gettin' kind of scared..."

Myra sighed, and Sandy pressed on.

"I reckon I'm going on about six months or so, an' my back is really givin' me a fit, tryin' to work in the truck stop an' all, an' I just need somebody t'help me. If I could find somebody...I wouldn't 'a called you, but..." Her voice trailed off, and Myra heard a soft sob before Sandy went on. "I-I ain't got nowhere to go."

Sandy waited for Myra's answer, a long time coming, while the jukebox king, Jerry Lee Lewis, picked it up after the turnaround, " —but I'll go through hell tonight if I don't see you—"

For all her womanly deferring to Wheeler and his everlasting, manly notions about everything, Myra had another streak that didn't show itself very often. Considering Wheeler with another woman, and her pregnant, lit a strange, cold fire in Myra. Anybody that knew her folks would have said the Tolliver was coming to the front. The Tollivers had a reputation for being tough as a herd of buffaloes from hell.

She hung onto the phone and pleated her apron against her knee, listening to Sandy's breath through the receiver. Wheeler. Wheeler's baby with another woman. Now the other woman calling to say she was scared....

Myra stood up, straightened her mama's picture there on the blue wall and cleared her throat.

"Sandy," she said, suddenly revived, "Tell me how to git to where you're at, an' I'll be there quick as I can drive it."

"You can just take 75 South to 41, an' the truck stop is right there at th' exit. I'll be in th' rest'rant part."

"Okay. Pack yore stuff."

"Pack my stuff?"

"Yeah, pack yore stuff. I ain't makin' but one trip."

Myra hung up and went back to the kitchen to latch the screen, lock the wood door and get her .38 revolver out of the pie safe. She spun the cylinder to make sure it was loaded and stuck it in her jeans at the small of her back, pulling her short, plaid shirt over it.

She moved easily through the small house, turning on the security light at the barn on her way to the kids' little lean-to room.

There was no hesitation in her voice as she commanded, "Git up, boys. We got us a trip to make."

## NIGHT RIDERS

The Diamond Horseshoe was a blaze of light. In Myra's words, "Lit up from hell to breakfast." She cramped the pickup in close to the building so she could see inside the restaurant. Behind the low counter was the woman she knew had to be Sandy—a great cloud of red curly hair around a thin face, a lot of make-up on her eyes.

*Good God,* marveled Myra, *she is pregnant. Big as a train.*

"Stay here, boys, an' I'll be on back in a few minutes." Roy and Barney, ages ten and nine, knew when mama meant business. They just nodded, and slid down in the seat of the pickup, indicating to their mama that they weren't even going to look.

Myra got out, ran her coarsened fingers over her skinny, jeans-clad rump and strode into the cafe. She walked straight down the long counter to the other woman, never taking her eyes off the pregnant waitress. When she was precisely opposite Sandy, she murmured, "If you got yore things t'gether, let's go."

A small, striped suitcase appeared on the counter, and Myra picked it up.

"This it?"

Sandy turned to the pass-through and announced, "Grady, I'm gone now. Be seein' you."

They walked out of the truck stop, Sandy a step or two behind Myra. When they got to the truck, Myra opened the passenger door, set the suitcase on the floorboard, and reached in to touch the boys lightly.

"Scrooch over some, now. This here's Sandy, an' she's goin' home with us."

*TELL ME ABOUT YOURSELF*

Once huddled in the pickup with her worldly belongings and three total strangers, riding through the night toward Georgia, Sandy had little choice but to surrender to her fate.

*I ought to be glad this woman come an' got me*, she told herself, *'cause I sure didn't have nowhere else to go. I don't know why, but I almost feel like I can trust her.*

*On th' other hand, my baby belongs to this woman's old man. Since I done confessed it, I don't guess I can take it back.*

Then, there was the matter of the revolver Sandy had caught sight of when they came out of the truck stop.

*Reckon she might want to use that pistol? If I was her, I bet I'd want to shoot me.*

It was then that she heard Myra's voice, surprisingly gentle, asking,

"Want some coffee?"

They had ridden in silence to Jennings, and Sandy suddenly realized that Myra had pulled off the freeway and into a bleak-looking service station.

"Oh, well, sure."

The boys were sleeping, piled together in the middle of the truck's bench seat. They didn't stir.

Once inside the station, Myra ordered two coffees. Turning to Sandy, she asked, "Need a doughnut? — eatin' for two makes a woman hungry."

They took the coffee and doughnuts outside and sat on the rusty drink box beside the door. Sandy kept looking at Myra in wonderment. Finally, she began to talk, to tell it all.

"See, when Wheeler first stopped at th' Diamond Horseshoe after I started workin' there, I thought he was th' best lookin' guy on th' road. That first time I seen him, I felt like he was th' man of my dreams. An' he kept comin' back, an' we kept on talkin' to one another, an' first thing you know, like, he's waitin' for me to get off work, an' all. Honest, Myra, I didn't know he was really married an' everything. He told me y'all wasn't livin' together, an' he swore you was gettin' a divorce. I mean, I believed ever'thing he told me. You know how that is, don't you?"

"Can't say as I do."

"Then, it got so I was just workin' with part of my mind, an' th' rest of it was thinkin' about Wheeler. I mean, honest, Myra, I was in love with him, an' I thought he was in love with me. I didn't know about you an' the kids an' all. Honest, I didn't. But, you know, I don't know how I would've felt if I *had'a* known. He was so sweet, an' so good to me an' everything. I do hate to tell you this now, Myra, but he, like, promised he'd make his insurance to me. That ought to show you how serious he was–how serious he sounded. To me, anyway. Myra, I didn't mean to do nothin' to hurt you. Nor them kids of Wheeler's. I was just crazy in love, Myra. I sure didn't set out to hurt nobody."

Then, that strange, fearsome silence. Myra kept biting into her doughnut and sipping her coffee. She squinted at the truck, at the gas pumps, at the moon. When she was done with the doughnut, she wiped her hands on her jeans and took a crumpled pack of Camels from her shirt, and a small throwaway butane lighter from a hip pocket.

Once her cigarette was lit, it still took awhile for her to respond to Sandy's confession. She just sat there, gently kicking the drink box, and smoking for a few minutes.

Sandy thrust hand and forearm deep into her crocheted shoulder bag and drew out a jumbo pack of Juicy Fruit.

"Want some gum?" she asked.

Myra shook her head.

"I never did learn how to smoke." Her tone was repentant for her failure to master an important skill.

Myra favored her with a quick, sidelong glance.

"It ain't no big thing."

"Yeah, well, but it looks like everybody in th' world smokes but me. But you know what, it's prob'ly better on the baby that I don't. Don't you reckon?"

Myra passed up the smoking subject in favor of more urgent matters.

"Sandy," she said, "we're two women who know Wheeler. At least one of us loves him. But we got to learn Mister Wheeler that a man don't git a woman pregnant an' walk away. Kids're too important. Far as that, pregnant women're too important. A guy can't do stuff like that an' git by with it. So me an' you are gonna set down an' figure out how to git Wheeler's attention. An' I'm gon' take care of you till you have that baby. If you want to keep it, well, it's yor'n to keep; an' if you don't want to keep it, I'll tell you now that I'll raise it 'cause it's Wheeler's."

"Oh, Myra. But, like, I already love this baby, an' I can't tell you how I appreciate all you're doing for us both. Tell the truth, I never thought about nobody raising this baby but me."

"Me an' you, though, we got to git along, not just for th' sake of yore baby, but for th' sake of my little boys out there a-sleepin' in th' truck. I'd be glad to kill somebody that messed with my boys, so let's me an' you work it out."

Myra slid off the drink box, signaling that this conversation was drawing to a close.

"Sandy, I got to tell you, if it wasn't for this mess we're all in, me an' you wouldn't never've seen one 'nother. But, now that we have, I think I'm gon' like you all right. We can git along as good as if you was my sister."

Sandy's relief at Myra's common sense was quickly replaced with worrisome thoughts of their other problem: Wheeler.

"Myra, what we gon' do with Wheeler? I mean, what 're we gonna tell 'im?"

"Tell 'im? Why, hell, girl, we gon' tell 'im th' truth. I can't think of no lie that'll cover it."

WELCOME TO OUR WORLD

Myra turned off the paved road at 4:30. At that hour of the morning, the lane to the house was hard to see, but she expertly whipped the pickup through the untamed underbrush and the deep, water-filled pot-holes for more than a mile.

Sandy's earlier fears resurfaced.

*Has this woman gone crazy? To be sure, Wheeler don't keep his family out in no wild woods like this jungle.*

Sandy bit her lip and tried to remember the few words of prayer her granny had tried to teach her. *Let's see, now: somethin' about layin' down to sleep an' dyin' before you wake up. Oh, Lord, I reckon that's how it's about to happen. God, I wish I hadn't ever saw Wheeler Boone. Nor no other man.* Then: *Maybe this is a short cut she's takin'. I know good an' well they ain't no house way out here.*

The sharper turn, the deeper hole and the jouncing pickup awakened the kids as Myra whirled up beside the porch and killed the engine.

"Mama, are we home?" asked Roy, untangling himself from his little brother.

"Anh-hanh." Myra pulled up the hand brake, and opened her door. "Come on, Roy. Git yore brother out an' let's go on in. Y'all got to go to school pretty soon."

Sandy pulled her sweater closer around herself and felt for the door handle. It looked as if this would be home. For awhile, at least.

Not until she got out of the truck did Sandy take in the premises. The house was small, painted blue with white edging around the windows and the front door. Thick clumps of pink azaleas in narrow, carefully-tended beds outlined the porch. The pitch darkness was pierced by a single security light on a pole by the barn, some hundred yards from the house.

"Git that suitcase, Roy," urged Myra, rounding the truck to Sandy's side. And, "Sandy, you wait right there till I kin git some lights on; I don't want you fallin' out here."

There was a flurry of activity as the boys clambered out of the pickup, took the suitcase and stumbled up onto the porch. Myra seemed to be in the middle of it all, giving orders and moving about with a certain clarity of purpose. Watching, Sandy felt the stirring of admiration for this woman who was Wheeler's wife. And her rescuer.

A ceiling light came on on the porch and Sandy could see a dirt path to the narrow, brick steps, a path that she took gratefully. The ride had tired her, and she felt bigger than a cow. She eased across the yard and up the steps, holding on to the porch post as she climbed.

Once inside the house, her heart sank. Although the place looked small from the outside, it seemed even smaller from the tiny living room. She could see on through to the kitchen, and knew it couldn't be more than five or six steps to the back door.

She heard Myra's voice in a room off to the left, talking to the boys about getting out their school clothes and collecting their homework.

*Just like hadn't nothin' happened out of th' ordinary! What kind of woman is she, anyhow?*

*WE KNOW YOU'RE USED TO BETTER*

"Sandy," called Myra from the other room, "if you got to go, they's a flashlight on th' counter by th' back door. The privy's right close to th' house—just watch yore step out there."

Sandy was stunned. *A privy? Great day, they didn't even have a bathroom in the house.*

She found the flashlight, and lumbered out of the house with as much caution as she could manage. The back steps weren't brick, like the front ones, but raw lumber laid across cement blocks, and they listed to the left a little bit. The need to relieve herself was greater than her fear of falling, and Sandy pressed on.

Safely back inside the house, Sandy found Myra at the stove, making breakfast with an expert hand; coffee was beginning to percolate, and a slice of ham was sizzling on a skillet. Turning from the pot of grits she was stirring, Myra nodded at Sandy and directed, "Th' plates are in that cabinet, an' forks in th' box there on top."

Sandy was setting the table when Roy and Barney came in, both looking sleepy, and eased into their chairs. Neither child spoke except to answer Myra's questions about the way they wanted their eggs cooked and, even then, their demeanor was tentative. The two women made some brief comments, but the tone of breakfast was uncertain and stilted.

*Things has got to git better than this,* thought Myra, *or I'm gon' go to eatin' mine outdoors.*

Once the meal was over, Myra got up, scraped the plates and stacked them in the sink. She reached for a man's jacket hanging on a nail behind the back door. "Let's git movin', boys; we can't afford to miss th' bus."

Then, "Sandy, go on in yonder an' lay down. I reckon you're right tired by now. I'll be back pretty quick."

They were gone. Sandy, alone in the blue house—alone in the world—thought about leaving before Myra got back. Only thing, she really didn't know where she was, and she could not imagine how she would go about finding the highway. Instead, she got up and looked through the house in search of "in yonder" where there was the promise of a bed. Sleep was what she really needed.

Three doors opened out of the living room; one to the kitchen, one to the room where the two children had been dressing and one that had been closed since they got here. Sandy tried it.

She'd never seen so much pink in one place. The walls were pink, the window frames, the bedspread, the throw pillows on the bed, all pink. The iron bedstead was just iron-colored, and the floor was bare except for a pair of small oblong rugs, one on each side of the bed. The rugs were flowered, but the predominant color was everywhere pink.

One window, overlooking the front porch, was draped with gauzy, double-layered, pink curtains that matched the bedspread. An oak dresser against a side wall looked like something grandparents must have left for a younger generation, and it was 'way too big for the cramped, pink bedroom. A pink curtain, floor to ceiling, hung catercornered across the opposite side of the room. That'd be the closet.

Sandy sat down on the bed, slid her sandals off her tired feet and eased back on the pillows. She was asleep at once, no longer caring where she was nor what her prospects were for anything better.

*SET AN EXTRA PLATE FOR SUPPER*

Myra came into the bedroom in the late afternoon and clasped Sandy's toes in her rough, square hand.

"You feelin' better?"

Sandy woke with a start, sat up and squinted her eyes against the late day sun streaming in at the lone window. It took a few moments to remember where she was, and to realize that the woman who was holding onto her foot was Wheeler's wife.

She looked up at Myra, half-expecting harsh words, anger, maybe a violent attack. What she got was a kind of tight smile.

"We gonna eat supper in a little while, Sandy. You missed dinner, so I reckon you needin' somethin' to eat by now."

Myra continued to hold Sandy's foot. Finally, she looked down at it as if she'd not seen a foot before. Truly, she never had seen a foot with the nails painted a brilliant, sparkling red.

The sight of the defiant little red toenails was somehow embarrassing to Myra as she realized that this woman had painted those nails for Wheeler's admiring eyes. Myra had never so much as considered painting her fingernails, and she couldn't imagine that Wheeler would have liked it if she had. Myra thought of her mother-in-law, Preacher Boone, who didn't hold with painting of the face, and wondered how she would take the sight of painted toenails.

*My God,* marveled Myra, *it's just one more pagan thing about Wheeler's woman.*

Supper was quiet, about like breakfast had been. Roy and Barney were the most subdued kids Sandy had ever seen. They both would flick a glance at her out of the tops of their eyes, now and then, but they really acted like she wasn't there.

The turnip greens and sweet potatoes were the best Sandy had ever tasted, and the pork roast was wonderful. The tea was dark and strong, sweeter than she was accustomed to. At Sandy's place, there was a small side dish with a sliced banana, smothered in sweet cream.

"That there bananer's gon' be good for you, Sandy; the rest of us don't need stuff like that." Myra smiled at her again, and this time the tight look around her eyes was gone. "It's been awhile since we had a baby on th' way, an' I got to remember what all's good for mamas to eat."

Roy and Barney exchanged a quick look, an identical understanding.

*So that's what it is!*

## MASTER PLAN

After supper, the kids went to their room and commenced to get their lessons for school the next day, and Myra and Sandy scraped the dishes and washed them. Sandy cleaned the oilcloth on the table and swept the tiny kitchen while Myra dried the dishes and put them in the cabinet.

"Come on in th' livin' room, Sandy," invited Myra. "Me an' you got to talk."

When they were seated on the blue naugahyde sofa, Myra reached for a little tablet of paper on the side table. Sandy could see that she'd already been writing on the first page. At the top of the page, Myra had written in a careful, round script, "Things to do for Sandy and the baby."

"I didn't see nary piece of baby clothes in yore things," she told Sandy, "so I reckon th' first thing is to git some clothes together for th' little feller.

"Me an' you can make most of 'em. I got a old machine out in th' barn, but it still works an' we can git th' boys to help us bring it in th' house. I can't see sewin' out there with th' cow a-watchin'..." She laughed at her own little joke, and her guest began to feel somewhat easier.

Sandy still suffered the sting of abject embarrassment, and she felt obliged to make an effort, somehow, to repent. And to thank Myra.

"Myra, I've wished a million times this hadn't happened. But I sure appreciate all you're doing. Like, I don't know what I would of done if it hadn't been for you. I wish I could tell you..."

Sandy's eyes filled with tears, spilling down her cheeks.

"You quit that cryin' now, Sandy. It don't matter none now. What we got to do is make th' best of it we can. What I been thinkin' is this: Wheeler wasn't to force. Now, was he?"

"We-e-l-l, I don't guess he was, at that. But I wasn't either, Myra. I tell you, every time he'd come struttin' in that cafe in his nice cowboy boots an' his pretty leather jacket, I'd nearly 'bout die!"

"Yeah, I bet," murmured Myra.

"You know, Myra, sometimes a woman gets to thinkin' she's queen of th' hill, an' she goes to believing things she knows good an' well can't be so. Like him bein' single an' all. Not that good-lookin' guy!"

"You think Wheeler's good-lookin'?"

"Ahn-hanh! Don't you?"

Myra drew a little doodle on her notepad, slid a moccasin off her foot and wiggled her toes. She appeared to be giving the question some serious consideration, and her answer was a long time coming.

"I really never thought about it, Sandy. I know one thing—if he ever had'a been, he ain't pretty to me no more! Now let's git down to th' list for that there little ol' baby or it's gon' be nekkid."

They sat there for more than an hour—two good-hearted, bewildered women, playing out the intertwined roles that a troubling fate had assigned them. When the list was complete to their satisfaction, Myra stood up, yawned and stretched, and commented, "I ain't been to bed since th' mornin' of that night you called. Was that just last night? Lord, it seems like a month…"

Then, "We ain't got but th' one bed, Sandy, so I reckon me an' you gon' have to sleep together. When Wheeler gits in, th' settee's gon' be his'n."

CO-CONSPIRATORS

Myra and Sandy stiffly occupied the bed, but they both slept without interruption until Myra rolled out the next morning at 5 o'clock.

"You go on back to sleep," she whispered to Sandy. "I got to git th' kids off to school."

Myra felt as if she and Sandy had worked out the details the night before, so she was ready to explain some things to the boys when they came in the kitchen for breakfast. They seemed to know that Mama had some news they had been wanting to hear, so they eased into their chairs and looked at her expectantly. When their plates were served, she took her seat at the table, reached a hand to each of them and set about explaining their situation.

"Roy an' Barney, Sandy in yonder is gon' have a little baby in two or three months. We gonna keep her here with us, an' help her git ready for th' baby. Y'all'll need to give us a hand, now an' then, an' I don't want to hear no complainin' about none of it."

Both children nodded assent, and both just sat there, not eating, not doing anything but trying to take in what their mama was saying.

Roy, being the older, spoke first. "Is she a friend of yor'n, Mama?"

Myra's steady gaze took in both pairs of brown eyes across the table from her before she answered, "Yep. She is, now."

TOWN HOUSE

As soon as she saw Roy and Barney safely on the school bus, Myra turned the truck toward town. This early in the morning, she could ride over Harlow and look to her heart's content—which is what she did. Up one street and down another, sizing up the houses that looked empty.

There was one at the end of Paglan Street that seemed about right; the lot was big and mostly overgrown, but the square, frame house looked sturdy. She liked its big front porch a whole lot, since it had banisters and some nice-looking, shallow steps at the side.

By 7:30, she had made a choice, and she drove back to the house to feed Sandy. On the way, she stopped at the 7-11 for a carton of orange juice. Startled at the price, she decided, *It shore better be good for her an' that baby.*

Back at the house, she re-started breakfast and called Sandy to get up and eat. For some strange reason, she thought about Hayden and wished for him to be there. *He could've brought that ol' sewin' machine in th' house an' not needed no help.*

When Sandy showed up moments later, Myra got right down to business. "You got any money?" she asked the pregnant woman sitting at her kitchen table.

"Well, let's see. I got $63 in my pocketbook, plus about $4.00 in change, an' I got last week's paycheck that ain't been cashed — it's about $184. It ain't much, but it's that much."

"That's all right. I got some put back, an' when Wheeler comes, he ought to have three or four hundred. I been puttin' some back every week since we been married, but I ain't never mentioned it to him. You know how men are. I let 'em keep my little savin's book at th' bank so nobody wouldn't find it. I'm goin' in there this mornin' an' see how much I got. An' me an' you gonna rent us a house up town."

Sandy clapped her hand to her mouth as if she'd been struck.

"Great day in th' mornin'! Can we do that?"

The pleasure she'd begun to feel at the prospect of living in town–bolstered by Sandy's obvious delight–beckoned Myra's thoughts toward unexplored avenues. It had been Wheeler's decision, and nobody else's, for his family to live in this isolated spot, cut off from everybody else in the world. To protect them, claimed Wheeler. Only now did Myra think to question what it was he meant to protect them from.

Even Hayden had said a time or two that Wheeler ought not to keep his folks out there where the living was "too hard for a pretty woman an' two plumb good young'uns."

*An' every time, Wheeler got mad an' said Hayden, hisse'f, was hell-bound an' he wanted everybody else to be th' same. Well,* she realized with some satisfaction, *Wheeler ain't callin' th' shots no more.*

*THE COLOR OF MONEY*

"You kin come on in th' bank with me, Sandy, an' git yore check cashed. Anyhow, you need to know what we're up against, an' how much money we gon' have to make it work."

They were parked in front of the only bank in Harlow. It was almost noon, and some of the folks going out of the stores to eat dinner spoke or nodded to Myra, all the while taking a look at the red-headed stranger with her.

Myra reached under the seat and came out with a tapestry bag; it had fancy, double handles that looked like rosewood to Sandy.

"What you got?" Sandy wanted to know.

"This thing's older'n me an' you put together," Myra said. "It belonged to my great grandma–call it a 'carpetbag.' We got to have somethin' to put th' money in."

When Myra got out of the truck, she went around to the other side to help Sandy out. "You don't want to fall, now," she warned. Together, they walked in at the bank's double doors, and Myra led the way to Frank Sizemore's office.

When Frank looked up and saw the two women, it took him a few moments to remember Mrs. Boone. She had never come in to see him, but he did notice her in the bank every once in awhile. She wasn't what he thought of as a regular customer.

He stood up and smiled, "Come in, Miz Boone." He waited for her to introduce her companion. He couldn't think if Mrs. Boone had a sister or not, but he could scarcely imagine that a sister of hers would be a fast-looking, red-headed item like that.

"Hey, Mr. Sizemore," said Myra. "You got my little savin's book here in yore office?"

*Oh, yes. It all came back to Frank Sizemore. This was Myra Boone, and she had been putting money into a secret savings account for years. Seems like she asked them to keep her book at the bank.*

It was always kind of odd to Frank, but he didn't dwell on it. As long as somebody was putting money in his bank, he just let them alone with their personal business.

Quickly, he grew effusive. "Why, of course, Mrs. Boone! Yes, indeed. Yessir, I do believe we're keeping your book for you. Yessir. Ah, let me call Juanita an' get her to fetch it for you."

When he was flustered, Frank Sizemore laughed. As he did now. "Yessir. Certainly!" He leaned outside the door and called a bank underling. "Lucy, tell Juanita to come in here for a minute, please."

Juanita came. Juanita, who had been at the bank for 19 years, knew everything that happened there; some said she knew every dollar in the bank by its first name. She did know, for instance, that Myra Boone had brought in close to $5,000.00 in the past eleven years, and that her saving account book was in Mr. Sizemore's bottom, left-hand drawer where she, Juanita, kept things the rest of the bank crew did not need to see.

While Mr. Sizemore did his nervous laugh act, Juanita strode into his office, opened the desk drawer and withdrew the account book. She handed it to Frank without comment, smiled at Myra Boone, nodded at Sandy and returned to her desk in the lobby of the bank.

"Well, now," Frank smiled, "let's see what's going on here with your account, Miz Boone." He laughed some more, thumbing through the small pages until he reached the latest entry.

"Well, ah, let's see, now. Ah, it says here..." he folded the book over and started again at the first page. "Ah, well. Ah, it looks like, ah...." He thumbed some more. "Like, well, about like you've got, ah, $4,897.12 in this one, little account, Mrs. Boone." He laughed some more. "Ah, I been thinking about you, Mrs. Boone. If you was to convert this to a C. D., we could come up with you some better interest on this little account."

Frank Sizemore was astute, laughing aside. He could smell the loss of deposited money in his bank. This time, the odor of money about to be withdrawn was strong in his nostrils. He had taught himself not to panic, though. Sometimes—well, once in awhile—they'd come on back. He just kept laughing, hoping he was striking a sincere note with this odd-lot pair of women.

"Is there anything I could do for you, Miz Boone? You know, I'm always ready to give my good depositors a hand, any way I can."

Myra took the book from his manicured hand and gazed at it for a good, long while. Then, she passed it over to Sandy, who looked for a somewhat shorter interval before handing it back to Myra.

"We'll take it," said Myra, pressing the carpetbag against his chest, "an' th' cash on this here check of Miz Whatley's."

*IF YOU GOT TH' HOUSE, WE GOT TH' MONEY*
Five minutes later, Myra and Sandy stepped into Harlow's only real estate office, two doors south of the bank.

Joe Lawton "Joe L." Hastings, who had been in real estate
since he was seventeen, looked away from the newspaper he
was reading to assess the pair of rough-looking females who
were invading his space.

*They don't want a damn thing but to jaw,* he concluded.

But he got up and met them at the counter.

"What can I do for you?" he asked, making certain that his
tone held no warmth.

"You know Paglan Street?" opened Myra.

"Yes, ma'am. Why?"

"They's a big, old gray house down there at th' end of th'
street an' a sign sayin' it's for rent. We're wantin' to rent it.
Today."

"That property belongs to Mr. Dorian Spells, a prominent
business-man. He only rents to tenants that can pay the rent."

Myra bristled. "We got th' money right here. How much?"

"He wants $300. That's every first of every month, rain or
shine, no excuses, no put-offs. If you can do it like that, I can
take the money and give you a lease for a year. You can re-
new it after that. That is, if you pay on time."

Myra pressed three new one-hundred-dollar bills into his
outstretched hand, reaching at the same time for the lease he
was holding. She scrawled her name with the pencil that he'd
offered and slapped the paper on the counter.

"We'll be a-movin' in tomorrow," she snorted, as they
turned to leave.

Sandy was laughing before they reached the curb.

"I thought you was fixin' to get a-holt of that little ol'
smart-mouth' jesse."

Myra nodded. "Look like he was a-beggin' me to. Th'
main thing is, we got us a house up town!"

# 2

# Movin' On Up To Th' Big Time

*SOFT-SHOD AND SENSIBLE*

Back in the truck, Myra braced Sandy with another new facet of their curious life together.

"We better go on by an' see Wheeler's folks. I don't want them to find out nothin' till I git a chance to tell 'em myself."

With that announcement, she lit out for Blue River community without waiting for Sandy's reply. Almost three miles out of town, Myra slammed on the brakes and slid the pickup around in the road, heading it back toward Harlow.

"I like to forgot somethin'!" she exclaimed.

Back in town, she slipped the truck into a space in front of the town's only dry goods store. Reaching for the carpetbag on the floor-board, she ordered Sandy, "Hurry up, now—we ain't got no time to waste."

Sandy, non-plussed, got out of the truck and followed Myra inside the store. She began to get the message when Myra dove straight for the shoe department, waved a sales clerk over and announced, "We got to see some shoes for her. An' we're in a hurry."

She motioned Sandy to a seat and went right on as if a shoe decision had already been made.

"It's gittin' hot weather, an' I think white's gonna be yore best bet. What size you take? About a eight?"

Myra turned back to the clerk. "Yep, I reckon about a eight. White. Somethin' that she can wear socks with."

Sandy couldn't think of some way to argue, so she let herself be shod to Myra's specifications. She never had liked to wear socks, but Myra ordered two pairs, and she accepted them meekly.

"She'll just wear 'em," Myra told the clerk as she handed over the purchase price. "I reckon you can put her old ones in th' box an' we'll take 'em with us."

The shoes were a two-fold victory for Myra. Sandy could now walk in comfort, and Naomi Boone would be spared the devilish sight of red-painted toe nails.

ₗIt was over in less than ten minutes, and they were back in the pickup. Sandy would have to admit that the white tennis shoes felt pretty good after her high heels, and all that walking–"all over hell's half-acre," as Myra put it. Sandy slid back in the seat and let the wind blow her red curls. It was almost like they were having fun.

*MEETING THE MATRIARCH*

About six miles from town on the paved road, Myra whirled onto a narrow, dirt road. It was in a lot better shape than the road to Myra's house; the trees grew close, but they had been trimmed back so that the limbs didn't scrape the sides of the truck. About a mile off the hard road, the forest gave way to verdant pastures on both sides of the road where sleek-looking, black-marked, white cows grazed in obvious contentment.

"Is that your in-laws' land out there?" she inquired.

"Anh-hanh, they got a big bunch of land out here, an' Merrill, he works like a pure slave keepin' it all goin'. He wants everything did perfect, but he's a good old man an' I like him."

"Has he got a lot of help?" Sandy persisted.

"Oh, yeah, he's got plenty of help. Every family in New Memphis has got somebody a-workin' for Merrill. Most of 'em had mamas an' daddies that worked for Merrill's daddy. Some of them — well, Mary an' Arlena an' Willie an' his two boys–they're second and third generation with the Boones.

"Now you take Willie — him an' Merrill's close as brothers. They was in th' war together, an' th' story is that Merrill lost his leg a-savin' Willie's life. He was a-tryin' to tote Willie off th' battlefield on his back when they both got hit with a grenade. Any time that's brought up, Merrill says it was a good swap!

"One thing, Merrill was th' first big landowner in th' county to make sure every black person on his place got off work to go an' vote. That's been somethin' like fifteen years ago, but folks still talk about it sometime. He went with 'em, hisse'f, that first time. When Merrill showed up like that, anybody that was a-meanin' to object just plain forgot to mention it. You would've thought Merrill figured up that there Civil Rights thing hisself."

"What's a 'New Memphis?'"

"Oh, that's th' name of th' community where Merrill's help lives. It's just across th' river; they used to be a ferry there 'til they built th' bridge. The same families has been livin' there ever since th' slaves was freed — I don't know how come they settled there. Just takened a likin' to th' place, I reckon. It's pretty down there, all right."

"What about Miz Boone? You like her?"

"Who? Naomi? Yeah, I shore do like 'er. She's th' uprightest woman I ever seen, but she's got a good heart. Only time I ever seen her lose it was when Hayden went off to prison. She took on an' hollered an' cried there for about a week; we couldn't do nothin' with her. One day I come over here an' Merrill told me she was gone; said she told him she needed to git by herself with God, an' she'd be on back when

God got through with her. An' you know, she come on back in about a week an' a half, bright as a dollar, an' I ain't never knowed her to cry no more since then. But, you know, she ain't been to see Hayden but one time, an' he's been in Reidsville goin' on three years."

"Don't nobody visit him?" asked Sandy.

"Oh, yeah. Me. I go about once a month. It ain't right for a man to be in prison an' believe th' world's forgot him. 'Specially if he ain't done nothin' much to be in prison about."

Before Sandy could assess Myra's faithful attention to her brother-in-law, they had turned in at a broad driveway and pulled up under the carport. The attached house was huge, painted white and richly embellished with Victorian curlicues. The setting was equally impressive; shrubs were trimmed and mulched like a nursery, and the yards — without a sprig of grass — had been meticulously swept.

A handsome, slight-built, older woman in a long, high-necked, black dress was rocking on the front porch, holding a book on her lap. The book turned out to be a pulpit Bible, well worn and replete with dark blue ribbon markers.

"Hey, Naomi, how you gittin' along?" Myra's voice was full of affection for their hostess.

Sandy followed Myra up the steps and onto the porch. By then, Naomi was on her feet, smiling in welcome. She hugged Myra, and then stood away to have a look at the stranger she'd brought.

"I told Merrill this mornin' I wished you'd come by. I ain't seen you nor the boys in a week or two. How've you all been? Ain't Wheeler got back yet?"

"We're all okay, Naomi, an' no, Wheeler ain't home yet. But sit down, Naomi, an' let me tell you how come I'm here. Or, how come we're here."

Naomi's eyes moved from Myra to Sandy, then back to Myra. Her face grew still, but steady and alert. She knew she was about to hear something she might not want to hear.

"Y'all want some ice tea?" asked Naomi, but she asked it as if she knew they had not come to drink tea.

Myra shook her head, pulled a rocker close to Mrs. Boone's, and motioned Sandy to bring a third one in closer. There wasn't any preamble at all. Myra just started talking, and Naomi sat still and listened.

"This other woman here is Sandy Whatley, Naomi. You can see she's pregnant. Th' baby she's gon' have belongs to Wheeler, an' I'm gon' look after her till th' baby's born. This morning I rented us a house up town, an' we're movin' tomorrow. She don't need to be 'way out in th' woods in case she gits sick; an' I think a pregnant woman needs a indoor bathroom."

Naomi glanced at Sandy, then looked back at Myra and murmured, "You didn't never have one when you was pregnant."

"That don't matter none now, Naomi. That's all in th' past. We got to look after her an' not be whinin' about what I didn't never have. You know how Wheeler was about livin' out yonder in th' country."

"You gonna need some money, ain't you? I'll get Merrill an' we can go on down to the bank..."

"Anh-anh, Naomi. See, I had me a little money put up, an' we gon' be all right, far as money's concerned. I just wanted you an' Merrill to know what's goin' on so y'all wouldn't be put out with me when you heard it from somebody else."

"Is they somethin' me an' Merrill can do to help you, Myra? You know we'd do anything in the world for you. How about some help to move? Willie an' his boys are here all the time. We can do without 'em for a day or so."

"Yeah, Naomi, now that's th' kind of help we can really use. An' another thing, we gonna have to give y'all th' cow, 'cause they don't let you keep a cow in town. Nor chickens, neither, I imagine. I was hopin' y'all would take 'em all off my hands."

Naomi got up and went inside the house and, a moment later, a farm bell started ringing. In a minute or two, a slender, black man rounded the corner of the house in a run. When he saw Myra he stopped, and smiled in greeting.

"Is Miz Naomi needin' me?"

Myra, who had left her chair and moved to the edge of the porch, returned his smile.

"Aw, naw, Raiford; she was just ringin' to see if you an' Willie an' Toby could leave this place for awhile tomorrow to help us move. We movin' in to town, Raiford—me an' th' young'uns an' Miz Sandy, here."

Raiford was quick to respond. "Yes, ma'am. We can go help you. Any time. We sho' can.

"Well, let's say 'bout 6 o'clock tomorrow mornin'. If we can start early, we can git through early."

Raiford agreed that early starting meant early finishing. All the while, he was puzzling over the presence of the red-haired woman. He had never seen Myra Boone in company with anybody but her husband and children; from what he'd heard Myra say, the stranger was living with them.

Myra put her arm around Naomi, who had returned to the porch.

"I reckon that's took care of. We shore thank all of y'all, Naomi. We got to go now. Got us a big, ol' yeller bus t' ketch up with. Come on, here, Sandy, let's ride."

As the two women were getting into the truck, Naomi called, "Myra, why don't you an' th' boys bring your friend there t'church Sunday?"

Myra froze in mid-motion. Obviously, the question put her in unfamiliar territory. Slowly, she turned to look back at her mother-in-law. When their eyes met, some unspoken covenant between the women took shape and Myra answered, "Thanks, Naomi. We—we might do that."

Back in the truck, Myra continued her Boone family history lesson for Sandy.

"Raiford, back there, he's one of Willie's boys I was tellin' you about. Him an' his brother, Toby, has been a-comin' to Merrill an' Naomi's ever since they was born. Growed up with Wheeler an' Hayden. Naomi loves to tell about Hayden a-cryin' when he was a little feller when he had to go to school on a different bus from Raiford. But, you know, they all got to ride together them last two years of high school. Raiford's mama, she says in them old days, Raiford spent more nights over there with th' Boones than he did at home."

"I reckon they're all grown an' married by now."

"Oh, yeah, Raiford an' Toby both. Raiford, he married a pretty little girl from Waycross, an' they got two young'uns. An' Toby, he got hisself a wife from over yonder around Cuthbert. Name of Colleen. She went to college an' everything, an' now she teaches school there in Harlow. They ain't got no young'uns. Not yet, anyway. I know she's th' best singer on th' place when Naomi has them conventions out here."

*PACKIN' UP, GETTIN' READY TO GO*

Myra raced to the school bus stop, slip-sliding around corners as if forgetting her passenger's delicate condition. Sandy held on and tried not to look as they whizzed past slower drivers, intimidating oncoming motorists and daring interference.

"Don't you suppose Roy and Barney would wait if you wasn't there when th' bus stopped?" asked Sandy, thinking Myra would take the hint.

"I ain't dependin' on it," muttered Myra, and kept on floor-boarding the pickup. "You don't never know who else'll be there with a taste for kidnapping little fellers like Roy an' Barney."

They made it to the bus stop a minute or two before the Bluebird eased off the road at the turn-off. Myra got out to meet the boys, and to open the tailgate so they could ride in the truck bed.

Back under the wheel, she craned around and hollered, "Y'all hold on, now, or I'll make y'all set up here with us."

Myra whipped the pickup out across the woods, once again unmindful of the hazards. Sandy wished one more time that she knew how to pray.

Finally, back at the blue bungalow, Myra stepped out of the pickup and reached over the truck bed for Barney, lifting him up and over the side. She hugged him briefly before she put him on the ground.

"Roy, you an' Barney go in yonder an' start puttin' all yore stuff in some of them boxes stacked up on th' porch. We movin' to town tomorrow. An' our help's gonna be here at six o'clock, so we got to be ready for 'em."

They whirled around and snapped to attention, eyes wide. "What's th' matter with Mama?" whispered Barney, tugging at Roy's shirt. Roy kept his gaze on Myra as he answered, "Don't ask me. Just do what she says." They struck out for the porch, hearing Myra yelling after them, "You boys git busy, now. We ain't got till Doom's Day!"

There was not all that much to pack. Myra brought two grocery boxes into the pink bedroom and started pulling down the curtains while Sandy rolled up the pink-flowered rugs. The two women worked in silence, with Sandy wondering if Myra felt any sweet sentiments connected with the bedroom. If she did, Sandy couldn't tell. Myra moved around and packed as if she'd never seen the contents of the room before.

When Myra yanked the pink curtain down from the wall to reveal the closet, Sandy marveled. Nothing of Myra's hung on the wire stretched across the corner but two pairs of jeans and a blue-striped cotton dress. The men's clothes were more plentiful—dress pants, white shirts and two sports jackets. There were three pairs of shoes on the floor, two of them Wheeler's. The others were Indian moccasins like the ones Myra was wearing then.

In the very back of the closet, on a nail, hung a long-sleeved navy blue knit dress with a white bertha collar. *That's a old woman's dress if I ever seen one,* thought Sandy. A paper sack in the back corner held a pair of black, low-heeled pumps that looked new. Seeing Sandy's obvious interest in the dress and shoes, Myra tried to be lighthearted with her explanation. "Them's my buryin' clothes, Sandy. I shore ain't got nowhere to wear 'em down here. Yessir, they gonna lay me out in that there blue dress an' them black shoes. I got th' low heels in case I have to walk all over God's heaven."

From the narrow closet shelf Sandy brought down a cardboard box labeled "Xmas decorations," and an opened carton of cigarettes. "These ceeg'rettes yours, Myra?"

"Yeah, they mine. Wheeler keeps his smokes on th' truck with him. That there carton was a Christmas present."

"Christmas? They ain't but two packs gone now!"

"Ahn-hanh. I don't smoke all that much. Mostly when I'm mad."

When they got through in the bedroom, Myra laid a hand on Sandy's forearm and smiled. "Now you want to see somethin' beautiful?"

Sandy nodded, and Myra led the way to the kitchen. Atop the cabinet where she kept the dishes was a cardboard box such as might have come from a woman's apparel shop. Myra pulled a chair against the cabinet and climbed up to retrieve the promised treasure.

She put the box on the table, untied what was surely old string, and lifted the top. She rubbed her hands together to assure herself they were clean before she reached in and brought out a flowered chiffon dress. It was cut low in the front, with tiny, cap sleeves; a soft, wide, matching sash was pinned with a tiny, gold safety pin to the neckline. The skirt was wide and double-layered. It was a real, honest-to-God party dress.

Myra was smiling, but her eyes sought Sandy's for confirmation that this was, indeed, a wondrous item of clothing—a genuine, womanly keepsake.

"I got married in this here dress," said Myra, gently fingering the sheer material. "I don't guess I had it on since then, but I always thought…" She didn't go on with what she always thought, but turned to Sandy and, shrugging her shoulders a bit, made the ultimate offer. "You want to try it on?"

A laughing Sandy admonished, "You must've forgot that I'm bigger than a bale of cotton with th' middle band busted."

"Oh. Well. Well, I just was thinkin' maybe, you know— maybe you'd, well—oh, hell, I don't know what I was thinkin'."

She folded the dress tenderly back into its flimsy cardboard hiding place, and carefully tied the string one more time.

"Let's try to keep this in th' pickup with us tomorrow. Merrill might send us a cow truck to move in."

Supper was swift and disjointed. As food left the plates, Myra swept them into the dish pan, washed them quickly and added them to the box that teetered on the edge of the table. Eating around the box was awkward, but there were no complaints. It was all so hurried that Sandy failed to notice that Myra didn't eat at all. She just washed things and packed.

She sent the kids off to bed as soon as they had eaten, and she and Sandy went on stripping the little house. The faded sampler that read "God Bless Our Home" was hanging too high to reach without climbing so, once more, Myra pulled a chair across the room for the needed height. She took the sampler down and, still standing in the chair, folded it twice and said to Sandy, "You can put this thing in th' trash. I don't reckon we'll be needin' it any more."

## AIN'T GONNA STUDY WAR NO MORE

By 5 o'clock the next morning Myra was back in the kitchen, having milked the cow and fed the chickens for the last time. She'd kept the coffee pot from the packing box, but had forgot to leave out cups and glasses. She put the pot on the stove and unpacked four coffee cups. The boys, she decided, could drink out of cups this one time.

Sandy came in the kitchen, yawning, trying to get into the day's events as best she could. She was tired, though. *Look like we couldn't get through last night,* she thought.

Myra took one look at her and touched her forehead with the back of her hand. "You got a fever?"

"Nope. I don't think so."

"Well, go on back in yonder an' lay down awhile. I'll bring you some coffee if it ever gits made."

Sandy lingered in the doorway as Myra turned back to the stove.

"Myra," she blurted, "when Wheeler gets here, I reckon you got a right to rail at him—but, you ain't gonna kill him nor nothin', are you? Tell me straight now, Myra. Are you?"

Myra took a long moment to face her friend. "Now, where would anybody git a notion like that? Why would I kill 'im?"

"Well, you got that gun. An' I know you madder than hell about what he done—what we done—an' I was just wantin' you to know I don't want to get mixed up in no killin'. Not if I can help it…"

"Go on back in yonder an' lay down, Sandy. Ain't nobody gonna git killed. I wouldn't waste good bullets on Wheeler Boone."

### WILLIE & WILEY & WONDERFUL

Just before six o'clock, Myra heard the rattle of Merrill's old cow truck out in the front yard. She stepped outside the door to see Raiford and Toby jumping down from the truck bed. Out of the cab on the driver's side came their daddy, Willie; from the passenger side stepped a young, white man Myra didn't know. He didn't look to her like the kind Merrill would hire to farm.

"'Mornin'," called Myra, "y'all are right on time."

"'Mornin', Miz Myra," called Willie. "Miz Myra, this here's Wiley Spells. He been helpin' Miz Naomi preach them sunrise meetin's at th' workshop. He was at th' house when we got ready to go, an' he say he could come help us."

*Good God*, thought Myra; *who'd git up to preach before daylight? I shore hope his strength holds out.*

"Howdy, Wiley," greeted Myra, reaching a hand out to the slender, dark-haired man. "We shore 'preciate any help we can git today."

"Glad to do it, Miz Boone," he responded. "Just tell us where you want us to start."

"You can start at th' front an' work yore way on through. We got everything about ready to go. Y'all want some coffee?"

They'd already had breakfast with Naomi, so they started moving furniture out of the living room and onto the truck. Wiley, Myra noticed, was certainly not slacking. He was the quickest one on the place. To herself she noted, *That boy shore can smile. Wonder is he like that all the time.*

She carried coffee to Sandy in the bedroom and whispered, "Sandy, they's a preacher out there, come to help us move. You better watch yore cork, girl." They both laughed.

"Watchin' a pregnant cork ain't hardly no trouble at all," joked Sandy, sipping her coffee. "Anyhow, what th' devil we doin' with a preacher out here? He think me an' you need savin'?"

"I don't know. But he's kindly pretty. 'Bout yore age, an' dang near 'bout yore size. He ain't no big man, but he ain't backin' up when it comes to movin' th' heavy stuff."

"You ain't answered my question, Myra. What's he doin' here?"

"I think he was over at Naomi's for that sunrise prayer thing she does on Saturdays, an' I reckon he was just tryin' to be a Christian an' come help some pore, pitiful women. That's 'bout all I can figure. 'Less Naomi put him up to it. She'll do that if she thinks it needs to be did.

"But you know somethin', Sandy? His last name is, 'Spells,' an' we're a-rentin' from a 'Spells' feller. I b'lieve they brothers."

"Maybe his brother sent him to see if we was fit for th' neighborhood. I hope we pass."

"Whichever way it went, I ain't sorry he come. Th' way we goin', we gonna be through 'fore suppertime."

Sandy put on her new white socks and her new white tennis shoes, and followed Myra into the bare living room. Everything was gone, already on the truck, and the moving hands were busy in the boys' room, taking down the bunk bed. She stuck her head in the door to have a look at the preacher. *Well, now,* she thought, *he ain't too bad to look at.*

"Come on in th' kitchen, Sandy," called Myra. "I can use some help with these chairs an' things."

Once Sandy was inside the kitchen door, Myra started to laugh. "Gittin' a eyeful of pretty boy? I told you to watch yore cork, but you wouldn't listen."

Sandy came close to Myra and murmured, "You was shore right! That boy's pretty as a pitchur. But, Lord, I don't want me no preacher."

"You could do a heap worse. With, say, somethin' like Wheeler Boone."

Embarrassed by her own candor, Myra sought to quickly change the subject. She flung open the screen door and yelled, "You boys git through tellin' that ol' cow good-bye, an' come on in here an' help yore mama an' Aunt Sandy. You hear me?"

*THE MATCHMAKER*

"We got th' firs' load about ready to go, Miz Myra. But we don't know where you was a-wantin' it took." It was Willie, standing in the kitchen door.

Myra pretended to consider a moment and then, "I tell you what: I need to stick around, but Miz Sandy can go with y'all an' show you where to put stuff. She'll be good as me, an' she can show y'all where th' place is at, an' everything."

She turned to Sandy. "You wouldn't mind goin' along, would you? I mean, I don't feel like I can git loose right now, an' they don't even know where th' place is at, nor nothin'."

Sandy grinned at Myra, letting her know that she was wise to the game. She turned to Willie and held up both hands.

"I give up. I can't say 'no' to her. Let's go."

By the time Sandy got to the porch, Willie had made arrangements for her to ride up front in the truck, and for Wiley to drive. He had assigned Toby to stay with Myra and help her with whatever she needed, and had taken his place at the back of the truck, ready to climb on when everybody else was in place. Raiford was already aboard.

Wiley got back out of the truck when Sandy appeared on the porch, and ran to help her down the steps. She accepted the offer of his hand, and managed to smile her appreciation. He maneuvered her around the jagged pothole close to the porch, and opened the truck door with a flourish. Sandy was impressed, but she thought again about watching her cork. *Myra ain't nobody's dummy, I'll tell anybody that.*

*Anyhow, preacher or no preacher,* Sandy decided, *Wiley Spells does seem a mighty nice man. Small, though. I like 'em a little bigger than he is. Wheeler, for instance, would make two of this guy.* She looked down at her distended belly and sighed. *Don't reckon he can help bein' small.*

Wiley drove the truck with expert care, easing it through the potholes and around protruding tree stumps, glancing at his passenger now and then as if to reassure himself that she was all right. Sandy tried not to let him catch her looking at him, but she let her gaze linger a moment too long just as they reached the highway, and he gave her a tender smile. She was surprised at his gentle expression, and some moments passed before she could return the unspoken bond of sweet conspiracy.

Once within the city limits of Harlow, she directed Wiley to Paglan Street and on down the dirt thoroughfare to the house. She pointed it out with a touch of pride in her voice, and was gratified to see his obvious approval of the big, square structure.

"I'll come back one day an' help Willie an' them get these yards shaped up," he offered. "It won't take too long to make it look nice."

Sandy was surprised to realize that she was happy about the prospect of seeing Wiley again. Especially recalling that, just a few nights ago, she had sworn off all men for the rest of her life.

*PAGLAN STREET PARADISE*

Willie and Raiford had brought brooms and mops and buckets and cleaning rags from Naomi's place, and they set about preparing the old house for its new occupants.

Sandy wanted to impress Wiley with their new, easy style of living, and he responded agreeably, nodding and exclaiming over each revelation as if he, too, had never been accustomed to such grand conveniences.

"It really looks like an ideal place," he said, "an' I'm so glad we're getting you all set up nice before the, uh, baby gets here."

He hadn't mentioned her obvious pregnant condition before, nor seemed to notice. Sandy blushed at the reference, and Wiley turned away quickly, pretending to be engrossed in removing a stain from the hall floor.

Willie was coming up the front steps carrying an old, high-backed rocking chair. He placed it on the porch carefully and called, "Miz Sandy, why don't you come out here an' set in th' rocker while we do th' heavy work? You can show us where you want stuff put from right here."

And so it went, Sandy in the rocking chair, telling each worker where she thought the meager household things belonged. Two hours after their arrival, the house was clean, the truck was empty and they were ready for the second trip.

The atmosphere had become easy and even playful. Jokes were made, and laughter drifted over the sparsely-settled neighborhood. Just before they had completed that first session, a short, dumpy, older woman had walked down from the next house—on the opposite side of the road and westward a good 300 yards away.

"'Mornin'," she called, "I been watchin' y'all a-movin' in, an' I come to tell you I'm shore proud to git some people in here. It's been darker'n th' bottom end of a well on this end of th' street ever since th' Morrises moved, an' that must've been a year or more."

"'Mornin'," answered Sandy, "an' I can't tell you how proud we are to be here. I'm Sandy. Don't you want to come on up on the porch and sit down? Willie can bring us another rocker up here."

"Naw, I ain't got time right now, but I'll be a-comin' back when y'all git settled in. I'll put a extra chicken pie in th' stove an' bring it for y'alls's supper."

Then, "Yore husband's a nice-lookin' feller. I bet he's proud 'a th' baby."

Sandy tried to smile, wondering how she could correct the error without disgracing Myra and her family. *Well*, she thought, *I can get that straight on down the road. No need to get here on the wrong foot.*

"I didn't get your name," she said to her visitor.

"Oh, yeah, I plumb forgot to tell you. I'm Vonceil Haggerty. Me an' my man been ownin' that nex' place up yonder since me an' him firs' married. That was goin' on 33 years since we bought it. Cost us eight hundred an' ten dollars, an' I bet it'd be worth ten thousand by now."

Sandy agreed as to the present worth of the neat, green house that she could see up the road. The picket fence, painted white, had caught Sandy's eye and her imagination when she first saw it.

"It sure is a nice place, Miz Haggerty. I'd love to come see it sometime."

Satisfied that her neighbors were reasonably tame and given to acceptable conversation, Mrs. Haggerty waved and turned back up the road.

"I'll see y'all after while," she promised.

# 3

# "Things Ain't What They Used To Be"

*LUNCH ON THE PORCH*

The next trip to Paglan Street was quicker and considerably easier than the first one. Myra, who had driven in with Roy and Barney and Toby behind the second load, congratulated her helpers for having done a first class job of arranging her new home.

"'Bout one more trip after this'n will do it," Myra told the group. "So why don't I go back down to Murray's Barbecue an' git us all some dinner before we unload that truck again? Me an' the young'uns is about to perish to death for somethin' to eat."

With that, Myra slid back into the pickup and took off, soon returning with a feast of barbecued ribs, corn on the cob, cole slaw, Texas toast and iced tea. Everybody gathered on the front porch for the midday repast.

There was much amiable conversation and easy laughter—to Myra and her children, a new and exhilarating thing—as they revisited the morning's adventures, and made further plans for improving both house and yard.

Throughout the meal, Myra took due note of Wiley's attention to Sandy; how he insisted that she relax in rocking chair comfort while he helped her plate, poured her tea, and fetched extra napkins. That's when Myra began to consider that Sandy's life might be greatly improved if she could be persuaded to stay right there in Harlow.

*My God*, thought Myra, *it's me that ain't wantin' her t'leave! I remember sayin' we'd be like sisters, but I didn't know I meant it.*

*LAST LOOK AND LONG GONE*

Long before sunset, the entire little group returned for the last time to the blue house in the woods. They walked through the place, looking again to make sure they'd left nothing behind. At last, Myra and the two children slipped from the house and made their way to the barn. Merrill had already sent for the cow and the chickens, and it all seemed eerily deserted.

"Mama, reckon we can ever have us another cow?" It was Barney, who had been unusually quiet while the moving was going on. "I bet Daddy's gonna make us git another'n quick as he gits here."

Myra knew what her son was thinking—that his daddy would be mad about the moving when he got home, and Barney envisioned Wheeler making them undo all that had been done.

"Barney, you ain't got nothin' t'worry about, son," she said, "we might git us another cow sometime, but we ain't got t'come back out here t'do it. An' we *ain't* comin' back, neither."

Back at the house, Myra drew her small writing pad from her hip pocket and a pencil from her shirt. Leaning down on the side of the porch, she composed a terse note for Wheeler to find when he got back. She'd thought a lot about what she could say without tipping her hand, and she had memorized the version she had liked the best.

The note, headed up with "Saturday," read, "Nobody lives here no more. We are at the end of Paglan Street in Harlow. You'll see the pickup parked out front." It was signed "M." It was the first time Myra had ever written anything to her husband.

It was like a party, that last trip from the old place and into town to the new one. Myra and the boys were squeezed into the cab of the pickup with the dress box, the deer rifle with its important-looking scope, the .22 rifle, the .12 gauge shotgun, the .45 Luger, the .357 Magnum, and Myra's own .38 revolver. Myra was sitting on the carpetbag.

Sandy, safe in the privilege of riding once more with Wiley in the cow truck, peered in at the pickup occupants and grinned.

"Looks like y'all are goin' to war," she teased. "I'd sure hate to meet up with you if I'd did somethin' y'all didn't like."

There was appreciative laughter all around, and even Roy and Barney took part in the hilarity. They hadn't quite settled on an attitude about this strange but agreeable disruption of their lives, but they both trusted their mother to do whatever was best.

Their two-truck motorcade moving down Paglan Street brought neighbors out on porches to watch, and to wave at the newcomers. Myra was liking all of it more and more, but she knew that Roy and Barney would be the final arbiters on the rightness of the move.

She need not have worried. Before they finished unloading the cow truck, the boys were making friends with Mrs. Haggerty's grandsons and the three O'Berry youngsters that lived just beyond the Haggerty place. She realized, with a kind of sadness, that her children had never had playmates at home in their lives. Living in that remote setting, despite the advantages that Wheeler claimed, had essentially cut them off from human contact. The boys weren't the only ones that had missed out on the comfort of friends.

Somewhat to her own surprise, Myra murmured, "Damn you, Wheeler Boone!"

## IF NOT TONIGHT, WHEN?

Myra and Sandy stood on the wide front porch to wave good-bye to Wiley and Willie and Raiford and Toby as they pulled away from the Boone's new residence. It was nearly sundown, but the moving was done and the house in reasonable order. Roy and Barney ran up on the porch to join in the waving. It had been a peculiarly invigorating day for all of them.

As they watched after the cow truck, they caught sight of a female figure on the road, pulling a coaster wagon and heading in their direction.

"Who's that a-comin' down thisaway?" asked Myra.

"That's our neighbor, Miz Haggerty," answered Sandy. "She's gonna bring us somethin' for supper, she said. She was up here this mornin' to see who all we was. They done lived up there in that same house for 33 years, she said. Imagine stayin' that long in th' same place."

Myra, newly mindful of the requirements of neighbors, tapped Roy on the head and told him, "Roy, you an' Barney run yonder an' help Miz Haggerty with th' wagon. Y'all behave now."

The boys took off in a run, meeting the neighbor and the wagon with just the right touch of friendly helpfulness.

"They got to learn about gittin' along with folks," Myra told Sandy.

Vonceil Haggerty had a sharp eye that she kept on her neighbors up and down the street. She hadn't yet concluded what was going on with the Boone family. She had thought at first that the good-looking young man was the husband of the younger woman, but he had left on that truck, so that must have been a wrong conclusion. And the other woman didn't seem to have a husband, either.

She could find out, though, from those two boys running toward her.

"Can we help you?" inquired Roy. "Mama said you might be wantin' us to help you."

"Shore can use me some help," she told them. "I was on my way to y'alls's house with a chicken pie an' some stuff for yore supper. Here; you can pull th' wagon. Be particular, now — that pie's hot."

Then, "Is yore daddy home yet?"

Roy felt hemmed in, somehow. He was not accustomed to being questioned about his family. Still, he had to answer.

"No, ma'am. We expect he'll git in tonight or tomorrow. He drives one 'a them big ol' trucks."

"Anh-hanh. Tonight or tomorrow, hanh? Well, I declare. Is the red-headed woman kin to y'all? I told J. B. while ago she kindly favors y'alls's mama…J. B., he's my husband."

Roy glanced over at Barney, making sure Barney wasn't about to say anything to this old woman that would hurt their standing as neighbors.

"Uh, well, she's our — our sister. I mean, our aunt. Mama's sister," lied Roy.

It was so easy. Emboldened by his small success, he tried another sip of that forbidden nectar with, "Her husband's outta town right now, but he's gonna be back pretty soon."

He didn't know exactly how he knew it, but he was certain that women who were going to have babies were duty-bound to have husbands. And Sandy, good a lady as she was, should not be left out.

Barney nodded as if confirming what his wise, older brother had reported to Mrs. Haggerty. He was glad Roy had been there, since he wouldn't have known he was at liberty to tell whatever sounded good.

Vonceil didn't leave it at that, though. When she stepped up on the porch, she fastened her gaze on Myra and commented, "Yore boys tell me yore husband is a-comin' in t'night, an' yore sister's ol' man's a-comin' in a day er two..."

Her eyes were watchful for some sign that all the truth had not been told. Ferreting out family secrets was something she did very well. It was just a flicker in Myra's eyes, but Vonceil caught it before Myra regained herself and acknowledged that both husbands would be home shortly.

*So!* thought Vonceil, *they's somethin' goin' on here that's needin' my attention. Well, it'll shore git it.*

Walking back up the road to her house, pulling the empty coaster wagon, Vonceil began to plot the least intrusive methods by which she might get all the dark details about her new neighbors. *Don't wanta spook 'em*, she decided. *Anyhow, I like 'em. To be shore, it can't be nothin' all that bad.*

After supper, Myra broached the subject that had hovered in the backs of all their minds all day.

"I reckon Wheeler'll be comin' in about tonight," she opened. "I want everybody to git settled down quick as you can now, an' let's try to rest. When he comes, I imagine we'll all git back up. An', Sandy, we got th' same ol' furniture, so you gonna have to sleep with me again."

They cleared the table and washed the supper dishes in record time, Roy and Barney lending a hand. The children were, by turns, glad their daddy was coming home and apprehensive about his return. It made them almost breathless with anticipation.

"Reckon he's gon' bring us somethin'?" Barney asked Roy, secure in the belief that his brother's saying it would make it true. Roy's response did little to ease his little brother's anxiety.

"Most likely whip us 'cause we moved to town. I dunno what he's gonna do to Mama." Seeing Barney's fright, Roy added, "But then, he might like it. I shore do."

"Oh, yeah, Roy. Me, too. Me, too."

## CHANGE OF LIFE

Wheeler wrestled the Peterbilt through the wooded trail that led to his blue house, easing the big vehicle down into the potholes and bringing it back up with caution, turning sharp in ways that the truck was never meant to do. It seemed like ten miles from the hard road to the house in the clearing.

The first thing he noticed was that the security light was not burning. It was dark everywhere–a strange kind of dark, one that felt deserted, a bit threatening. He let the truck lights burn as he climbed down to the ground and moved toward the porch. As soon as he could get the porch light on, he'd go see about the security light.

*Wait a minute! Where's my pickup?*

He started running toward the house. There wasn't a glimmer of light anywhere. He opened the door and reached inside for the light switch before he realized that the house was empty, and the power was off. Startled, he just stood there for a moment, trying to get a grip on what was happening. He didn't know why he did it, since it was clear that nobody was there, but he called, "Myra! Myra!"

Back outside, his eye caught the flutter of a piece of paper under a rock on the edge of the porch. He picked it up and hurried back to the truck's headlights where he read his future.

Suddenly, Wheeler's total self—mind, body and soul—was suffused with the blistering blaze of angry surprise.

His response was typical Wheeler Boone: *What th' hell?! What does she think she's doin'? By God, I'm th' one to say when*

*this bunch is movin' somewheres else! An' ain't nodamnbody
movin' nodamnwhere.*

He and the Peterbilt re-traced the tedious route back to the
highway and set out for Harlow. Wheeler rehearsed his fury
on the way. *Myra – that damn quiet little black-eyed Cherokee
savage, Myra – always actin' like she was mindin' me so damn
good. One thing's goddam certain: we gonna move on back home
tomorrow.*

Wheeler checked his watch to find that it was 2:30 A.M.
*Well, no, by God, we'll move on back home today.*

He found Paglan Street and strained his eyes for his
pickup that was supposed to be parked by wherever it was
he was going. At the end of the street, just like the note said,
he saw it parked by the porch of a big, square, gray-painted
house. There were no lights on these strange premises, either.

*Just as well go on in an' git it over with,* he thought, guiding
the Peterbilt past the pickup and onto the grassy patch
overlooking a stand of pines on the north side of the
property.

*SHOW TIME*

Myra knew that Peterbilt and its powerful whine. In the
hush of night, hearing it was no trouble at all. She recognized
it when it turned onto Paglan Street.

"Sandy, you 'wake?" She touched Sandy's shoulder. She
wanted Sandy and herself to be at their brightest when they
confronted Wheeler.

"Lord, child, I ain't been t'sleep, yet," answered Sandy.
"That's him an' that ol' mons-ster truck, ain't it?"

"Anh-hanh, that's both of 'em. You can tell 'em apart all
right–th' one that's hollerin' 'll be Wheeler."

They giggled softly, and Myra reached for Sandy's hand.
"Be stout, now, Sandy. We got to do this just like we
planned."

Getting down from the truck, Wheeler's anger, which had gained momentum on the ride to town, reached fever pitch. Secure in the certainty that he had been done wrong, he meant to prove that he would not take such things lying down. Somehow his manly rule about not cursing in front of his boys abandoned him in his hour of need.

They heard him stomp onto the porch and into the living room.

"Myra! Goddammit, Myra, where you at? By God, I mean to git some goddam straight-assed answers, by God. You hear me, Myra? This is yore goddam husband a-talkin' t' you, you crazy-as-hell sleazy cross-eyed redskin bitch!"

Wheeler was loud, and Wheeler was so furious he felt ready to explode. He was not accustomed to neighbors around his house, but he didn't care if everybody in Harlow got up to hear his complaint.

"Goddam crazy hay-headed sonuvabitchin' bitch," he yelled. "A goddam hard-workin' sonuvabitch can't even go t'work without some loonytick bitch takin' ever'thing he's got an' parkin' it in some goddam shanty in some hellhole town! By God, Myra, you better hope t'God you don't keep on 'til you make me hurt somebody. Can't you nor no other goddam bitch git away with stompin' Wheeler Boone's ass! Myra! You hear me, bitch? You git yore bony ass ou'chere an' face th' fuck up to what you done! I done takened all the goddam hell-hackin' I'm gonna take offa you."

"Yep, he's shore riled," Myra whispered, "a-cussin' th' cross out. I hope Miz Haggerty don't think to call th' po-lice."

Storming through the house, turning on lights and yelling, Wheeler found the dining room, the kitchen, the back porch. Back through the hall, he flung open the door to the darkened bedroom where Myra and Sandy waited.

He slammed his hand against the wall, searching for the light switch. When he found it, he jammed it upward.

There, sitting up in bed and smiling, smiling the way somebody smiles at a stranger, was his wife — *that crazy, bitchin', cross-eyed, hay-headed, redskin savage heifer, Myra, and oh, sweet Jesus! Sandy Whatley!*

The fury died. Wheeler Boone–hard-working, truck-driving family man, Wheeler Boone–had met his match; had been bested by a pair of women. He was done for. He resented with all his might that they had the galling guts to smile as he was going under for the third time.

He fell back against the doorjamb, mouth open, wordless. His breath stopped. Time stopped. Maybe his heart stopped for a brief span of time as he stared at the two women. Then he slid to the floor with a mighty thump.

Neither woman seemed to notice that he had fallen.

Myra spoke first, inquiring brightly, "You hungry? We got somethin' left over from supper if you want us to heat it up."

Wheeler stared across the room at Myra and her bed partner. Finally, he shook his head and stammered, "I–I ain't h-h-hungry," as he scrambled to his feet.

"Well, you got a blanket an' piller out yonder on th' settee. I reckon you 'bout ready to git some rest."

Silence. Nothing but silence. Myra adjusted her thin frame as if to resume her interrupted sleep, and Sandy followed her lead.

"Well, we'll see you in th' mornin'," Myra said softly. "You wantta put out that there light?"

## *I DIDN'T SLEEP A WINK LAST NIGHT*

Wheeler's mind, more accustomed to uncomplicated turns, whirled. The critical questions tumbled about in his head, making him feel a trifle seasick. But there were no answers for such as: How did Sandy and Myra get together? Who paid for the house up town? What happened to the boys? Why did Myra do all this without even telling him, say nothing of asking?

He could reach but one conclusion: *She's crazy! That's it — pure, stark, ravin', outta-her-damn-head crazy! IN-sane!*

Wheeler lay down on the settee. He thought about taking off his boots, but he didn't have the strength. Neither did he have the strength to sleep. He lay there a long time, staring into the darkness.

Finally, his seething mind devised a plan of sorts. He got up and went again to the bedroom, flipped on the light and addressed Myra in the most coldly formal tone he could muster. He hoped she noticed that he didn't let his eyes even glance Sandy's way.

"Where're m'pickup keys?"

Myra turned, sat up and shook her head, rather the way she would refuse if one of the kids made an outrageous request.

"I can't let'cha have em, Wheeler. We gonna be needin' th' pickup to go to church this mornin'. I reckon you could unhook yore trailer an' drive bobtail if you was a-needin' to go somewheres."

Her words sounded so reasoned, even with his knowing that she'd never set her foot in a church-house since they married. *Damn her to hell*, he thought.

"Well, I was needin' to do some things—haul some things."

He knew he sounded weak, and the realization rekindled his rage. But what could he do? Out-done again, he turned to leave.

"Th' light, if you please, Wheeler. We tryin' to git some sleep here."

### TERRORS OF TOWN

In the menacing darkness, Wheeler Boone unhooked the trailer from his tractor. *Hell–that's where I've landed–hell, where them damn two bitches decided to put me while I was out tryin' t'make a goddam livin'.* His mama's face danced through his shocked mind's eye–*how many times have I heard her a-goin' on about th' wages of sin an' eternal hell? I just hope she'll find out what them two women has did to me. They're th' goddam sinners.*

Wheeler's mind slid, pressed him to the brink of screaming. A nameless fear began to rise in him, suggesting horrors never before entertained. He heard curious noises, phantom footsteps stalking him, voices of the imps of purgatory whispering in the night.

Some desperate scoundrel was out there, watching him. He knew it; could feel alien eyes peering at him through the fog. Any minute, a pair of criminal hands would lay hold on him; a gun barrel would touch the back of his neck, a heedless finger would pull the trigger...

Wheeler kept shaking his head, as if to clear the miasma that had settled in his brain. He had to think.

Once the tractor was free, he pulled himself up and into the driver's seat. That, at least, felt familiar. It would soon be morning, and he could work it all out then.

Driving away from the house on Paglan Street made more noise than had ever been noticeable when they were at home in the country. Wheeler thought about who might live on the street, and wondered if they were accustomed to the aarrrrrrrrmmmmmmmm of a Peterbilt tractor tearing out in the night. Not that he cared–he hoped to God they didn't like it.

*Mess with me,* he threatened his suddenly hostile world, *an' I'll just haul this here damn rig right on back to Macclenny. By the time he reached the intersection, another basic desire had taken hold of Wheeler: he was thirsty. Hold on, now, maybe I need a damn*

*drink of whisky, mor'n anything else–a drink, an' a bunch of fellers*
*to gimme some back-up.*

LAUGH, AND THE WORLD LAUGHS WITH YOU

When they were sure he had gone, Myra and Sandy
turned the light back on in the bedroom and began to laugh.
They entertained each other with mimicry of the Wheeler
scene.

"Didja see him when he turnt that light on?" Myra
gurgled, pausing in mid-sentence to fall across her knees and
go breathless with mirth.

Sandy held both hands over her pregnant belly and
laughed until she was hoarse.

"An' how 'bout that fallin' down he done? Weren't that a
sight for somethin' big as he is t'do?"

"Oo, yeah! He went ker-WHUMP! Put me in mind of a
dang elephant a-fallin' over. That's what he done—ker-
WHUMP!"

Tears of triumph rolled down both their cheeks. Talk
about sweet victory! They had really got the best of a dang
fool man!

It was hard to stop making fun of Wheeler. He had
brought it all on himself, and they figured he deserved every
moment of their unchecked ridicule.

Roy and Barney heard it all, lying in the darkness. Roy
had crawled down from the top bunk to lie beside Barney
when they first heard Wheeler's semi driving in. They hadn't
known what to expect, for their fears had grown since
suppertime when Myra said he'd be coming home that night.

They had heard Wheeler's boots hit the porch, heard his
wild, vile, profane tirade; they had cringed when they heard
him approaching their mama's bedroom. They would not
have been too surprised had Wheeler killed them all.

They had heard him, too, when he got up from the settee and went the second time to their mama's room. That time they really feared the worst. Nothing happened–just him going out of the house and unlinking the trailer from the tractor and driving away.

And then they heard their mama and Sandy laughing like they couldn't stop. Barney couldn't help giggling when they just kept on heehawing in there, and Roy was sorely tempted, himself, to join in the derision of his father.

All in all, it was a strange night, unlike any of them on the place had ever experienced.

When the house was quiet again, Roy disentangled himself from his little brother's anxious grip and started to climb back to his own section of the bed.

Barney caught his sleeve as he was reaching and whispered, "Roy, are you gonna hafta go to hell for tellin' that ol' woman that there lie about Sandy a-bein' Mama's sister, an' all?"

"I hope not. But if I got to go, ol' lady Haggerty ortta hafta go, too, 'cause she ort notta ast me."

Roy settled back down beside Barney to consider his chances of going to hell. But Barney had some other questions he needed to have answered.

"Roy, is Mama cross-eyed?"

"Anh-anh. He just said that 'cause he was mad."

Barney wasn't quite ready to let go. He clung to his older brother for just one more assurance.

"Roy," he pleaded, "let's me an' you don't never act like that. Hear, Roy?"

Roy reached over to pat the thin little shoulder.

"Don'chu worry none, Barney. We ain't!"

Long after the boys were asleep again, Myra and Sandy lay awake. They were as stunned as Wheeler by their victory.

"Myra," said Sandy, "I didn't know you was a Indian. Wheeler said you was. Are you?"

Myra laughed. "Lord, girl, I dunno. Some of 'em said that my great-great-grandma was about half a Cherokee, but Wheeler told me he didn't want that to git out, or folks wouldn't have no respec' for him."

# 4

# Win Some, Lose Some

*ON THE GLORY ROAD*

Four pairs of curious eyes confronted Naomi Boone from front row seats as she mounted the pulpit on Sunday morning. Naomi, being the pro that she was, seemed to accept the quartet as part of her regular flock. She smiled benignly at each of them before she began to read her text.

"Th' Old Testament Book of Ruth speaks to our hearts this morning," she began. She was in her preacher voice, precise and tempered, revealing her upscale education.

"Naomi said, 'It grieveth me much that the hand of the Lord has gone out against me' —

"'And Ruth said, Intreat me not to leave thee, or to return after following thee; for whither thou goest, I will go; and where thou lodgest, I will lodge; thy people shall be my people, and thy God my God; Where thou diest, will I die, and there will I be buried;

"'The Lord do so to me, and more also...'"

Naomi paused, let her gaze rove over the gathering and, in an entirely different tone and in the vernacular, she bellowed, "Lissen t'me, brothers an' sisters, she's a-sayin' she's a-wantin' God t'smite 'er down —"

Back to the Bible and her pulpit persona, Naomi concluded the passage in a soft, dramatic voice, emphasizing key words, "…'if ought but death part thee and me.'"

Naomi had read with passion, bringing her eyes to rest again and again on her daughter-in-law who sat, rigid and scarcely breathing, as she beheld her mother-in-law at work for the first time.

When she finished her text, she closed the Book and fastened her gaze on Sandy, who was also visibly taken aback at the power of the preacher woman's voice and by the very presence she had assumed there in the pulpit of a country church.

"Like Naomi of old," she intoned, "I have a daughter-in-law; her name is Myra, but in truth, she is my Ruth.

"Not many days ago," Naomi told her congregation, "my daughter-in-law sat beside me on my front porch and related a sad story of a man gone wrong. That man is my son."

Myra gasped audibly, and Sandy reached for her hand.

"You didn't tell me she'd spill everything from th' pulpit," she whispered.

"I didn't know she would," Myra murmured.

Naomi ignored the two women and their discomfort, continuing with her sermon.

"The hand of the Lord had been raised against me, and against mine," she said, "but even as He chastises us, His love abides.

"In the past few days, we have welcomed into our family the stranger who has suffered the most from my son's misconduct. My daughter-in-law, mindful of the devices of the Lord, has opened her heart to this woman stranger and has pledged herself to her service.

"On my knees in prayer, I have asked—and will continue to ask—that my daughter-in-law be strengthened by the very love she has offered to one who some might see as her rival.

For the Lord rewardeth the righteous, and provides balm to a broken heart that never wavers in His service.

"My son–Wheeler–wherever you are this morning, I pray God will press hard against you for your sins; will punish you according to your misdeeds and, by His Mighty Hand, bring you back into His fold before you leave this vale for the Land Beyond.

"But, my son, if you turn away from the Lord, and fail to hear His holy admonitions, I'll not plead with Him for your sake in this world nor the next."

Naomi stood there, straight, calm and still. Her congregation, as one, fought the temptation to stir. Roy looked down at his little brother to see if he was crying. He was. Tears gushed from his eyes and rolled, unchecked, down his cheeks. As badly as Roy wanted to comfort him, he just continued to watch the waterfall and never moved at all.

"The Lord go with you to your homes and command your hearts in all the days to come."

Naomi lifted her eyes to the heavens and turned from the lectern, signaling that the service was over.

She walked past the flabbergasted front row foursome and moved on to the back of the church for the traditional greeting of her people. Not one of them made mention of the specifics of her sermon, but there were many expressions of support.

"I'm a-prayin' fer ya, Naomi," was the most common one. And one or two went so far as to say, "If I kin do airy thing fer y'all, just lemme know."

### IN TIME OF TROUBLE, EAT

Myra and her group continued to sit in their pew, uncertain about leaving, uncertain about staying, and especially uncertain about how they would ever face Naomi again.

She came back for them when the others had gone.
"Y'all come on to th' house. I left Mary an' Arlena cookin'
a plumb feast. I told them y'all would be eatin' with us.
Merrill's all worked up about us all bein' together again."
*What kind of woman was she?* Sandy was truly puzzled at
the way Myra's mother-in-law was behaving. Of course, she
had not had much experience with preachers, but she had
them all figured some other way.

Myra stood up and motioned Sandy to go on ahead of her;
she reached out for the boys, and the five of them walked
wordlessly out of the church. They climbed into their
respective vehicles and set out for Naomi's house.

In the pickup, silence reigned. Roy dried Barney's eyes
and wiped his face with his handkerchief, feeling protective
and grown-up, and Barney leaned his head against Roy's
shoulder. Neither of them cared for this adult situation, but
there wasn't any way out of it.

Sandy stared ahead, not once fluffing her hair or sliding
her bracelets up and down her arm. Naomi Boone had
rendered her stone-still.

Myra's mouth took on that little quirky pinch at one
corner, the way it did when she was dumbfounded. She
drove with an unaccustomed measure of caution and, from
time to time, she glanced at her passengers. To her mind,
everything that needed saying had been said.

*COME LIVE WITH ME AND BE MY LOVE*

Dinner at the Boone plantation turned out to be
memorable. Naomi and Merrill had been warmly interested
in all the plans Myra and Sandy had devised for living up
town, and even the children relaxed in the glow of family
fellowship. There was no mention of Wheeler.

Sandy's estimate of the older Boones grew to unexpected heights; she sat back, from time to time, just to revel in their hospitality. To think—these were Wheeler's parents!

Back at their new home that afternoon, Roy and Barney were sent off for a nap while Myra and Sandy repaired to the front porch rockers for another planning session.

"I hated to mention it around th' young'uns, but did you notice Wheeler come got his trailer while we was gone?" Sandy knew before she asked that Myra had noticed, but she really wanted to talk about how they could avoid Wheeler altogether.

"Yep, I noticed," answered Myra, "but that don't mean a thing. Maybe he had another run."

"But, Myra, what are we gonna do when he takes a notion to come back?" was Sandy's next question.

"I ain't shore, exactly, Sandy, but I know one thing: he ain't gon' tear up nothin' me an' you done worked out. We got to git busy on them clothes for th' baby, an' we ain't got time for none of his fool cuttin' up."

They rocked a few times before Myra went on.

"Wheeler's a-doin' what my daddy's oldest sister, Aunt Lessie, used to call, 'a-playin' firefly.'"

"Doin' what?"

"A-playin' firefly, Sandy. What she meant–'scuse my language–was he's been a-showin' his ass an' holdin' us a light to see it by."

The earlier tension eased as the two women sat giggling at the wisdom of the old folks. Soon, though, Myra turned back to the main subject.

"I'm shore glad we got th' ol' sewin' machine in that there spare room back yonder. They's plenty of room to work in. An' I was thinkin', we can go git us some furniture for that room an' then you can sleep in it. I bet you wore out tryin' sleep with me..."

"Yeah, an' I bet you tired of havin' a big ol' ox in bed with you, too." laughed Sandy.

"Okay, tell you what: tomorrow we'll git th' young'uns off an' then we'll go on up town an' buy us a bed an' some things; an' maybe they can bring it on down here 'fore they close up tomorrow evenin'."

As they sat there, a small, new car drew up at the front.

"Who you reckon that is?" Myra was half expecting Wheeler to pull in.

"Looks like Wiley a-gettin' out," offered a sharp-eyed Sandy. "Walks sort of like him..."

Myra eyed her housemate. "I see you been payin' attention to how Wiley walks! What you reckon I'm gonna do with you?" Myra was laughing and Sandy was grinning back at her.

"Just because a woman's watchin' her cork don't mean she can't watch somethin' else at th' same time," retorted Sandy, laughing as she gave Myra's arm a little slap.

They turned their eyes toward the male figure crossing the front yard. It was Wiley, sure enough. He waved when he saw they were both looking his way.

He stepped up on the porch and went first to Sandy.

"How you feelin'? The moving didn't get you down, did it?"

Sandy liked the way he looked straight into her eyes when he spoke to her.

"Oh, it wasn't too bad. We've been tryin' to rest some since y'all left yesterday."

"Come on in here an' sit down," urged Myra. "Pull that other rocker around here—I'll let you sit by Sandy."

Wiley did as he was told, bringing the chair close to Sandy's side. He rocked back as if taking a sample of the chair's comfort.

"These're some good rockers y'all got here," he offered. "I bet you can't buy rockers like this any more."

"Yeah," agreed Myra, "them was all Naomi's rockin' chairs she give me–give us–long time ago. They been out yonder in th' barn ever' since. Till we moved in here." They soon exhausted the subject of rocking chairs, and Myra rose, moving toward the door.

"I'm gonna go make us some tea. Y'all just sit here an' talk, an' I'll be on back after while."

When she was gone, Wiley reached out to Sandy. After a moment's hesitation, she placed her hand in his.

"Sandy, I know we just met yesterday mornin', an' I've been tryin' to understand how you feel about th' way things are goin'. Since I never do believe I got all th' sense a man ought to have, I been out to Naomi's this afternoon to talk with her. She seems to think I'm on th' right track. You see, by the time I looked at you yesterday, I knew where my heart was. Maybe I ought not to say 'I love you' all this quick, but Sandy, that's th' way I feel. Am I a fool?"

Sandy looked down at her bulging front, and then off across the yard. She felt tears start, but she didn't want to cry. So she just kept rocking, not saying anything.

"Sandy, I reckon that all came out wrong. I was just trying to explain...don't cry, Sandy. I wouldn't make you cry for anything."

"Why, I ain't cryin', Wiley. Really, I ain't. I mean, what would I want to cry about?"

"Well, maybe I come on too fast, too strong. But, Sandy, I do love you."

They both rocked in silence for a few minutes, but Wiley was afraid to let it last too long.

"Sandy—Sandy, I'll just go if you think that's best."

"You ain't got to go, Wiley. It's just that I'm gonna have another man's baby. Or hadn't you noticed? You're, like, too good a man to get mixed up in this mess."

"I'm not 'mixed up' in anything. If you'd let me, I'd love that baby like it was my own. I'm trying to tell you I'm ready to love you long-term. You an' th' baby."

"I don't see how I can let you do that, Wiley. Thank God, I got Myra to help me get through this. I mean, I can't see pullin' you into it, too."

"Sandy, can't you see it's what I want to do?"

"Yeah, Wiley, I see. Ain't no man of yore stripe never loved me before, an' it would sure take some gettin' used to. What makes it so bad is, well, I'm afraid I love you, too."

He quit the rocker and fell on his knees in front of her, reaching to hold her.

"Your arms ain't long enough to go around all this," murmured Sandy, laughing a little.

"Darlin,' darlin'…"

Myra stepped out of the screen door at that moment.

"Ah, hmmm. Well. I see y'all been gittin' acquainted," she said, resuming her place in her rocking chair. "We'll have us some ice tea in a few minutes an' y'all can cool off."

From his kneeling position, one arm still around Sandy, Wiley turned to Myra.

"Myra, what do you think about me asking Sandy to marry me? Do you suppose that would be all right with you?"

"Well, ain't you gonna ask her first? Then you can ask me. I might as well tell you now that I ain't gonna go against it in no way."

"Sandy? Will you? Will you marry me, Sandy?"

"Oh, Wiley. I will. You know I will."

*WHAT'S YORE DADDY'S NAME, CHILD?*
Dwight Monk was glad every day that he'd persuaded his aristocratic wife, the former Lorraine Selwyn Galway, to move from her family's Charleston estate down to Harlow, Georgia. He knew she missed the opulent South Carolina society that she had been brought up in, and he was mindful of her sacrifice.

Still, Lorraine busied herself with civic betterment, rather like a devoted missionary sent from the Mother Church to the wilds of darkest Africa. Between her inherited money and Dwight's considerable income, they lived like royalty in these lesser climes.

Dwight never apologized for his extraordinary intelligence, his enviable education nor his elaborate lifestyle. He even kept his political ties quiet. He was a man at home with himself.

The clients who kept him in fat retainers were corporations his home county clientele never heard of, and he saw no reason to advertise his corporate dealings. He enjoyed the confrontations with the other local lawyers before the circuit judge, and he delighted in securing the rights of his charges in and around Lolacolola county.

Naomi Boone was one local who had never sought Dwight's advice for herself before that Monday morning. She was parked in front of his office when he came down just after eight o'clock.

He had met Merrill Boone the first day he'd been in Harlow, and he liked the old man; he liked his preacher wife even better. She had sent many a client to seek his counsel, and he'd always managed to come through for her flock.

"Good mornin', Dwight. Do you have a few minutes? I have a problem that needs all th' help you can give it."

"Why, of course, Mrs. Boone. I hope I'm never too busy to spend time with you. Come on in."

And to his secretary, Pearl Hadsock, "Hold my calls, please, Pearl."

He escorted Naomi into his private office and closed the door. Naomi took the chair that Dwight indicated while he selected a handmade, Cuban cigar from the humidor on his desk, snipped the end with a silver cutter and lit it from the teak-clad desk lighter.

"Now, Mrs. Boone. What can I do for you?"

Naomi had rehearsed her speech, and she laid out the details of Wheeler's infidelity, Myra's rescue of Sandy, Wiley's intention to marry Sandy before the baby was born.

"Here's th' big question," she said, "who is that baby's daddy? I mean, legally? An', do you reckon Wheeler could go to court an' take that baby away from Sandy an' Wiley?"

Dwight was genuinely surprised at the bizarre circumstances that this woman had laid out for his consideration. *How in the hell could she tell all that to him? To anybody? And without a trace of embarrassment! That's what comes of being righteous,* he decided.

"Well, does Wiley want to claim the child?" he inquired.

"Yeah, that's what he tells me. An' Sandy wants him to, too."

"Okay. Here's the way the law goes, Mrs. Boone. When a child is born to a woman who is married, the law presumes that the husband is the father of the offspring. That is, if Wiley and Sandy marry before the child comes, Wiley would be the presumptive father.

"BUT: if Wheeler wants to contest the paternity, he has that right. Any judge will require blood tests of the baby and Wheeler. If the test results show that Wheeler is the father, the court will so rule. Of course, then Wiley could seek to adopt the baby. First, he'd have to show that Wheeler is not a fit and proper person to have the child. Then it would be necessary to prove that he, Wiley, in accordance with the court's rather stringent guidelines, is fit and proper. It could get ugly if Wheeler decided to contest the paternity, but ultimately, Wiley might prevail."

Naomi took it all in.

"Any other time, I'd say I wouldn't *let* Wheeler show out like that, but right now, I don't know what I can do with him. Really, he's acting crazy."

"Tell me what you want me to do."

"Nothing, right now, Dwight. I'm gonna try to get Sandy an' Wiley married quick as I can, an' we'll go from there. I appreciate your good help. If Wheeler tries to get that baby, I want you to represent Wiley. I'll pay you, myself."

Almost as an afterthought, she asked, "Did you ever hear anything about Hayden?"

"I'll be talking to the governor day after tomorrow, Mrs. Boone. I think we'll have some good news soon, especially since the judge promised me he would go along."

*I'LL MEET YOU ON THE OTHER SHORE*

When Naomi turned off the highway onto the road home, she was confronted with an EMT wagon racing toward her with lights flashing, siren screaming. The driver recognized her and skidded to a stop.

"Mr. Boone's in here with us, Miz Boone. Had a heart attackt out at th' milkin' barn. We're on th' way to th' hospital."

He thrust his vehicle in gear and plunged on toward the highway, and Naomi whipped her car around to follow.

"Lord," she prayed, "if Merrill's got to go, please look after him 'til I get there. An' I want to thank you for all them sweet years I had him; especially for lettin' a man good as Merrill love a ol' fool like me. I loved him back, Lord–You got to know that. An' I still do, but if You want me to try to get along without him, I'll do my best."

Merrill was already dead before they left his house, but the EMT's just couldn't tell her. They would leave that to Dr. Marshall, who was waiting at the emergency entrance. He stopped briefly to confirm that life had left Merrill, and walked quickly over to Naomi's car before she got out.

"Miz Boone," he began, "I'm afraid..."

She touched the hand he'd laid on the door frame. "I know, Dr. Marshall; he's gone, ain't he? I knew it when I met them with him. They wasn't no life a-comin' outta that wagon."

After a brief pause, "If you don't mind, would you call th' funeral home an' tell them I'm on th' way around there to see about buryin' him."

She started her car, patted the doctor's hand and drove around the EMT wagon to the street back toward town.

*BAD NEWS TRAVELS FAST*

Word of Merrill Boone's death flew across Harlow and Lolacolola county like wildfire. Long before Naomi completed the final arrangements, the funeral home was filled with friends and neighbors. Merrill's final hours were told and re-told, and soon everybody knew that Naomi had not been with him when he died. That circumstance gave even more cause for mourning and head-shaking.

"Good as she loved him," began the most oft-told recounting. And, "I don't know how she's gonna get along without him..."

Naomi kept glancing up to see if Myra was there, but Myra hadn't heard.

Late that day Vonceil Haggerty stepped up on Myra's porch carrying a sweet potato pie. Sandy answered her knock at the door, and Vonceil could tell that this household had not got the news.

She put her arm across Sandy's shoulder and began, "I come t'tell y'all I'm sorry as I can be about Merrill an' all..."

Sandy drew back, puzzled.

"What about Merrill?"

"Oh, y'all ain't heard? Child, Merrill's dead. How come somebody didn't come tell ya?"

Myra emerged from the kitchen, still unaware.

"Is that th' fellers with th' new furniture, Sandy?"

She quickly realized that something was amiss when Sandy turned to her.

"It's Merrill, Myra. Miz Haggerty says he's dead."

Other footsteps hit the porch; this time, it was the furniture delivery men.

"Might as well come on in with it now," Myra directed, easing Vonceil and Sandy out of the doorway. "You can put it all in that there second room down yonder on th' left. Just set it anywhere an' we'll git to it later."

She led the way to the kitchen and the three women sat down at the table. They sat in silence for a few minutes until Vonceil spoke.

"Is they somethin' I can git y'all? Somethin' I could do fer ya? I hear they done got Merrill at Gaston's, but I don't know where Naomi is right now. They tell me she went right on around there an' made his funeral arrangements quick as she found out he was dead."

Myra shook her head at Vonceil. "No'm, thank you. I reckon we'll go on out yonder to Naomi's an' see about her. I got to git th' young'uns in th' house an' tell them about Merrill."

The delivery men appeared in the kitchen door, announcing that they had set the new pieces in the designated room and were about to leave. Myra let them go as she headed for the back porch to call Roy and Barney. Furniture was the least of her worries right then.

Half an hour later they were in the pickup, heading for the Boone farm. Roy and Barney had cried briefly when they were told of Merrill's death, and had subsided into their silent mode before they left the house. One more shocking event seemed almost natural to them, considering the past week.

Cars and pickups were streaming out of town toward the same destination, and Myra crept along in the traffic, trying to come to grips with what had happened. It was as if her world — the familiar, safe place she thought she occupied — had disappeared the night Sandy called her and since then, everything associated with her ordinary life had fallen apart and lay in pieces at her feet.

She had to park a good way from the house since cars and trucks were everywhere. People milled about on the porch, and the house was filled to overflowing. Every light on the place was burning.

"Looks like a convention," she whispered.

Sandy was unsure of her role in all this, and she drew Myra aside.

"Listen here, Myra, would you rather I'd just stay out here an' let you an' th' young'uns go on in? I don't mind. Y'know, I never even seen Merrill but that one time–yesterday at dinner–an' folks might think I was, like, tryin' to horn in."

Myra turned to face her. "Wait out here? Anh-anh, Sandy. If I ever needed a true friend, I need one now. I ain't up to givin' a damn what nobody thinks tonight."

The two women and the two children kept on walking toward the porch. Roy and Barney had slipped between the two women when they stopped to talk, and now both children's hands were being held by an adult as they made their way across the broad lawn.

A tall figure stepped in their path, blocking their way. It was Wheeler.

"Where th' hell you think you're a-goin', heifer? Ain't nogoddambody sent for you. Nor for that slut you got with ya. All of ya git off my land rightgoddamnow so I won't hafta hurt none of ya."

Wheeler was drunk.

Myra and Sandy exchanged long looks, Myra glanced down at her two children, and the four of them turned away, retracing their steps. When they reached the pickup, they piled in without a word and Myra ferried them back to the highway.

Dead Merrill or no dead Merrill, Wheeler was still their biggest problem.

# 5

## Timing Is Everything

*THE CONSPIRATORS*

Willie had seen and heard the confrontation between Wheeler and Myra's little troupe, but he could not figure what, if anything, he could do. In the midst of his own, deep grief over Merrill's death, he would have preferred not to have been on hand for that ugly scene.

Still, Myra was his friend, and so was Sandy. They were pretty much alone in the world, as far as Willie could tell. If it weren't for Naomi, he didn't know what might happen to them. He realized he'd always disliked Wheeler. At times, he had tried to dispute it to himself, but he knew that it was true: Wheeler, beneath all his hard-working family man exterior, was a selfish, willful, hard-headed bully. And lately, Wheeler had become dangerous.

As he leaned against the live oak, a small car pulled in beside Naomi's workshop that she'd fixed up for prayer meetings. He recognized Wiley Spells's little vehicle, and he ran toward it, bent on catching the young reverend before he went in the house.

Wiley seemed glad to see a familiar face. "Hey, Willie. I wasn't sure where I should go, or anything. I really wanted to see Naomi, but I know she's got friends in there with her that she's known lots longer than me. I sure don't want to intrude."

Willie brushed aside Wiley's doubts, and began to relate the grim scene that he had witnessed. Wiley listened intently until Willie had gone through all of it.

"He didn't hurt them, did he, Willie? Where did they go? Did you see which way they went when they left?"

"They didn't give him time to do nothin' but what I told you. They just turnt 'round an' went on back to th' truck an' got in and left—they didn' act mad nor nothin', just left when he told 'em to leave."

Wiley clasped Willie's hand. "Thanks, Willie, thanks. I expect I'll be needin' your help before this is all over, but right now I need to get in th' house an' see Naomi. But I sure don't want to run across Wheeler. Do you know how I can do that?"

"Come with me," Willie told him.

He led him down the back slope and up again to the back porch that opened into the kitchen. Mary and Arlena were there, tearfully preparing food for the swarm of people who would likely stay through the night, and making a tray of tea and muffins to be taken up to Naomi.

"Lord, I hate what we got to face now," mourned Arlena in rhythmic cadences. "I don't know if Miz Naomi can carry on without Mr. Merrill—seem like she ain't as strong as she used to be. And she sho' did depend on him—Lord, yes, she did—but not no more...he's gone."

Wiley took it all in, wondering if any of this branch of Naomi's family would ever accept him, a stranger to the group, even though he loved Naomi as if she were his mother.

Mary looked up when he came in, easing his fears a bit with, "I'm sho' glad you here, preacher. Miz Naomi thinks a lots 'a you, an' I 'magine she been a-wantin' to see you."

Willie, however, directed his remarks to Arlena, the older of the two and the acknowledged bosswoman of the household.

"You reckon we can get Mister Wiley up yonder to Miz Naomi's room without runnin' him into Wheeler? That boy been showing out tonight–drunk as a man can get."

Arlena cut an appraising look at Wiley, back to Willie, and down to the bowl of cake batter that she was stirring. She wasn't yet certain of Wiley Spells's place in this family. He hadn't been back from preacher school long enough for her to get to know him, but Naomi took to him as soon as he'd appeared on the premises.

Quite suddenly, she made a point of getting elaborately busy there in the kitchen, firmly turning her back on the group and noisily pulling pans from wall cabinets. All the while, she was weighing the possibilities: *If I help him up yonder t'see Miz Naomi, an' she don't want him there, Arlena gonna be at fault; if I don't help him an' Miz Naomi do wants to see him, Arlena sho' gonna be did wrong.*

With some reservation, Arlena decided to help Wiley. That Willie, she must concede, had been on the place longer than anybody else, and he seemed to approve of Wiley.

"Tell you what, Willie: he can come with me when I take her tray. I uses th' back stairs, myself, an' ain't no Wheeler gonna be aroun' there. He never did like them back stairs, even when he was a child. They was too dark."

*WE'LL GRIEVE LATER*

When the tray was arranged, Arlena and Wiley slipped out of the kitchen and mounted the steep, narrow staircase. Arlena, he guessed, was probably sixty years old, but she moved about with unhurried grace, always doing, always helping. *Why, of course,* Wiley said to himself, *she's living the*

*Christ life! I'm going to use her life as an example in some sermons–I hope she won't mind.*

Several family friends stood about in the upstairs hall, some of them crying, all of them looking mournful. Naomi's door was closed. Arlena swept through the crowd, sliding past several of them with a murmured "'Scuse me, please ma'am..." and a polite "We just needs t'come th'ough. We brought Miz Naomi a little supper..."

Quickly maneuvering through the assembled mourners, Arlena tapped at the closed door and slipped inside, bringing Wiley in in her wake.

Naomi, fully clothed, was lying back on a high, four-poster bed, pressed against a mountain of pillows. She opened her eyes when she heard Arlena's voice, and smiled at her black friend. When she caught sight of Wiley, she sat up.

"I been wonderin' where you was at, Wiley. I feel like I been in here a week without a face I really wanted to see. Come on over here an' sit down."

Then, "Arlena, you sure fixed somethin' nice for me to eat. Tell you th' truth, I was gettin' hungry. Merrill wouldn't think we was helpin' him by starvin' ourselves, would he?"

Satisfied that Naomi was in good company, Arlena bowed out and went back down to the kitchen to continue the food preparations.

"Naomi," began Wiley, "I really didn't know Merrill as well as I do you, but I know your heart's broken. Th' Lord moves in strange ways–we all know that–but I'm here to bring whatever comfort I can because I care about you."

He held her strong, bony hand in both of his, and she gave him a tender, smiling nod.

"I know, Wiley, an' you can't ever know what your bein' here means to me. You would've loved Merrill if he could have stayed around awhile longer. As it is, you and me got to go on, Wiley. God's got somethin' for us to do or He wouldn't have let us stay."

She sought his eyes as she asked, "How 'bout Sandy, Wiley? You still wantin' to marry that girl an' claim that baby?"

"I went to see her yesterday afternoon, Naomi, an' she's agreeable. So is Myra. An' I'm more determined than ever. Naomi, I love that girl. She's everything I ever want in a wife."

"Good, good. We better get busy on some weddin' plans, hadn't we?"

"Naomi, I know time is runnin' out. Wheeler is here, tonight, here on th' place, an' I'm sorry to tell you, but he's actin' bad. He ran Myra an' Sandy off–they were here with th' young'uns, an' he made them leave. Did you see him?"

"Wheeler's here? No, I didn't see him. He hasn't said a word to me. Wiley, is he drinkin'?"

"'Fraid so, Naomi. No man would talk to Sandy an' Myra like he did if he wasn't bad drunk."

Naomi was off the bed, taking one more sip of her tea. She clasped Wiley's hand and pulled him to his feet.

"We better move, Wiley. Where's your car at?"

"Down by th' workshop."

"Then, come on, boy. Let's go to Myra's house. We better try to get y'all married tonight."

## PREACHERS ARE FOR MARRYIN' & BURYIN'

At the door, Naomi turned and dashed back across the room to the telephone. As she picked up the handset, she was leafing through the slender Harlow directory.

"Here we are," she said, and punched some numbers on the instrument. "Hello? Tracy, lemme talk to yore daddy. This here's Naomi Boone."

When her party answered, Naomi did not waste any time with the amenities. "Lester, I need you to go back down to your office tonight. We got to have a marriage license, an' I'm talkin' right now."

She paused for his response, mashing her mouth into a straight line and rolling her eyes at Wiley in mocking irreverence at Lester's officious balking.

"Anh-hanh. Tonight. I'm at home, but we'll be up there time it takes us to drive it. We leavin' quick as we can get in th' car."

To Wiley, she nodded vigorously and urged, "Let's go, Wiley. We ain't got all night."

The two of them eased out of her door, Naomi murmuring to the tearful gathering as they passed. They tip-toed down the back stairs, out the kitchen door and across the dark backyard to Wiley's car.

"Don't cut your lights on unless you just got to have 'em," Naomi warned. "We don't know who's out here lookin' thisaway."

Wiley took her orders without bothering to question anything she said. Her next order was most welcome.

"Go on by Myra's an' let's get her an' Sandy."

Myra and her entire brood were on the front porch. Roy and Barney sat on the steps, whispering over a sack of marbles Myra had bought them the day before. Myra and Sandy occupied the rocking chairs. From time to time, Sandy sighed, but no word came from either woman. Wheeler's attack had been so unexpected–and so brutal–that they had run out of words.

Both of them knew it was Wiley's car that stopped in front of the place, but they continued to sit in silence. When they saw that Naomi was getting out of the passenger side, they both got up and started toward the car. Sandy rushed to Wiley's outstretched arms, and Myra embraced Naomi.

"Oh, Lordy, Naomi, I hate it so bad–Merrill, he was a good man, Naomi–Lord, I know you gonna miss him. Far as that, we all gonna miss him. Is they anything any of us can do for you?" Myra tried to convey her sympathy to Naomi, not really noticing that Naomi did not seem to be actively grieving at that moment.

"It's all right, Myra, honey, I know you loved Merrill. An' yes, we all gonna miss him more than we can tell right now. But th' Lord's got things for me to do, Myra, an' I mean to do them. He's seein' after Merrill–I'm confident of that–an' He expects me to tend to what He's laid out down here."

She turned to Wiley and Sandy, holding each other there in the darkness, and reminded Wiley, "Better tell 'em what we gonna do, Wiley. Time is a-runnin' out, son."

Wiley told the women of Naomi's plan to have a wedding that night. He recounted the call to the probate judge and how he and Naomi had decided on the way to town that the ceremony would take place in the workshop.

"I ain't got no weddin' dress," lamented Sandy.

Myra turned from the group and ran to the house. She quickly returned to the porch, scooped up the children and raced back to the car. She was carrying the box that held her own wedding dress from years gone by.

"We'll make this do for a weddin' present if we can't do nothin' else," she promised.

## YOU GOTTA HAVE A LICENSE

The six of them, pressed close in Wiley's little car, headed out for the courthouse. For a wedding party, it was exceedingly solemn.

Lester Carlton was waiting, puzzled, avid for the details of whatever Naomi Boone had in mind on this night when her husband lay a corpse. Lester had always looked upon Naomi as, perhaps, a creature from another world. She intimidated him, and he felt obliged to comply with whatever she wished. His puzzlement grew when he was presented with the prospective bride and groom. The bride was noticeably pregnant and the groom was that young preacher-brother of Dorian Spells.

*Good God,* he thought, *I used t'think them Spellses was above such as this.*

Reining in his curiosity, he peered up at the bride-to-be and began the requisite bureaucratic questioning.

"Name?"

Sandy turned to Myra with a rueful smile.

"I reckon you gonna find out somethin' else about me now. I'm sorry I ain't told you before." Then, to Carlton, "Elmer Cleo Whatley," she said softly. "Everybody calls me Sandy, but it ain't really my name. Or Sandra—I just like Sandra."

Lester Carlton's pen had not touched the paper when Naomi interrupted. "'Sandra' will do just fine, Lester. It's her chosen name, an' that's the one you can use."

Lester followed Naomi's instructions without looking up.

"Age?"

"Twenty-one an' a half."

"Birthplace?"

"Lafayette, Louisiana."

"Parents' names?"

"Elmer Fred Whatley an' Cleo Laura Simmons. They're both dead, like my granny that raised me."

Then it was Wiley's turn, and he spat out his statistics without hesitation. Sandy, Naomi, and Myra learned that his first name was actually Wildwood, his middle name was Corbett, and that he was twenty-four years old.

"You folks got your blood test results with you?"

Naomi was ready for Lester before he ever turned the page.

"Lester, you just leave all that blank, an' we'll tend to it later. You got my word on that. What I want is a marriage license, an' that's what I mean to get."

He sat there a long moment, weighing his official duty against some unspecified retribution that Naomi Boone surely had the power to impose on him. He was more afraid of her than he was of what any measly State regulatory board might get around to doing.

Presently, he handed the marriage license, complete with his official seal of office, to Naomi, since she was obviously in charge of this ragtag bunch. *Better her than me*, he mused.

"How much we owe ya, Lester?" she asked.

"Ah, 'bout $22.50, I reckon."

"Here." She handed him a $50 bill. "Just keep th' rest for comin' down here tonight. An' thanks, Lester. We'll try to remember you when you have to run again."

*IF YOU WILL PROMISE ME*

"Take me back to git my pickup, Wiley," Myra said when they were back in the car. "This thing's a mite crowded. An' anyhow, me an' these young'uns gonna want to git on back home before mornin'."

Back to Myra's house, letting three passengers out and on to Naomi's, Wiley kept his peace, but he was still apprehensive about Wheeler's possible interference with their plans.

Naomi knew his thoughts, and she, too, spent that time considering how to handle an unruly, drunken Wheeler. Merrill's face danced across her consciousness, and she could have sworn he was smiling.

Back at the Boone farm, Willie was waiting by the workshop. He stepped out of the darkness as soon as they parked.

"He's in th' house, Miz Naomi, tellin' some of them folks about Miz Myra a-leavin' him an' goin' off with Miz Sandy. He say he don't even know where they at."

"Go back in yonder, Willie," directed Naomi, "an' see if you can get him to go to bed. Tell him I've gone to sleep. An' you can tell everybody else th' same thing. I ain't got time to be worried with any of them right now. Then you get on back out here with Mary an' Arlena because we'll be needin' some witnesses for th' weddin'."

Before he could get more than a few yards away, Naomi called him back. "One more thing, Willie, tell Arlena and Mary I said to put some clean sheets on th' bed in th' room that used to be my mama's–we're havin' overnight company."

*God Almighty! She do mean to have a weddin'. An' she gonna let 'em stay in her mama's old room. She ain't let nobody sleep in that room since Miz Dickerson died.* Willie ran, trying to come to terms with all of it. *Lord have mercy,* he thought, *I sho' wisht Mr. Merrill was here.*

*I NOW PRONOUNCE YOU...*

The workshop was really a little chapel with a dais opposite the main entrance and a lectern positioned in its center. A huge, lighted cross dominated the platform where two high-backed chairs graced opposite sides of the lectern.

"We can't turn on many lights," warned Naomi, "but we can light candles. That'll be a nice touch, anyhow." She handed a box of kitchen matches to Roy and motioned Barney to help him do the lighting honors.

They stood around in a cluster, nobody but Naomi knowing exactly what to do. She busied herself in preacherly preparations at the front of the room, glancing up now and then to look toward the door.

Presently, Willie, Arlena, Mary, Raiford, and Toby slipped quietly into the chapel, all looking alert and expectant. Naomi came at once to them and asked, "Did y'all see Wheeler?"

Willie shook his head. "No'm, I don't know where he's got off to."

Naomi just nodded and began doling out duties.

"Raiford, you an' Toby stay right outside th' door an' don't you let nobody in here. If Wheeler comes down here, you better not let him in. Knock him out if you have to. An' Willie, you gonna be my assistant, so come on up yonder with me. I want Arlena an' Mary to stand with th' bride an' groom as witnesses, an' Myra's gonna be matron of honor. Roy can be Wiley's best man an' Barney can give th' bride away. Then he can escort his mama to her seat after he does his stuff.

"Y'all come on, now. Let's do it."

Naomi moved smoothly through the ceremony, pressing her charges along with great dignity. The common denominator throughout was tears: Sandy wept copiously, as did Myra. Wiley cried without a trace of embarrassment; Willie cried, Arlena cried, Mary cried, Roy and Barney occasionally fell to sobbing. Outside, Raiford and Toby, who could hear the proceedings clearly, tried without success to stem the tide of unaccustomed tears coursing down their dark faces.

By flickering candlelight, Elmer Cleo "Sandra" Whatley became the bride of Wildwood Corbett Spells. Amen. They were safe from Wheeler for a time.

"All we got is some communion wine," said Naomi, "but I reckon we can all have a sip a' that for celebration. Maybe we'll get a chance to do better one day soon."

# 6

## The Light That Failed

*HONEYMOON SUITE*

It was late when Myra and the boys got back to the house on Paglan Street, and they were ready to wind down after a night of such high excitement. Roy and Barney almost fell asleep while their mama was getting them into their pajamas.

Myra went back to the front door to make certain it was locked, and then checked the kitchen door. It was a ritual she had taken up since they moved to town just two days earlier. It was not a stranger that she feared—it was Wheeler. Still, the thought of Sandy and Wiley eased her mind. They were so happy and so right for each other.

Myra had begun to like planning–a thing she'd never done much before Sandy had come into their lives. Tonight, sleepy or not, she felt excited about her plans for the following day.

At breakfast, Myra told the boys, "Y'all tell your teacher that your gran'daddy's dead, an' that y'all ain't gon' be at school tomorrow. I'm lettin' y'all go today because I believe you gonna be just as well off there as anywhere. Maybe better. But y'all tell her what I'm a-tellin' you, you hear?"

As soon as Roy and Barney were gone, Myra went into the room where the new furniture waited. She was glad the delivery men had set the bed up. The chest of drawers and the vanity that she and Sandy had chosen were standing in the middle of the big, airy room and the drawers were stacked on the bed. Bedside tables were upended on the bed, too.

By noon, Myra had all the furniture in place to her satisfaction, and had brought a lamp from the living room to put on the vanity. It looked nice. They had forgotten to buy bed linens, but the other thing they'd forgot was of utmost importance. *I'll just go by there,* thought Myra, *an' bring it on back, myself.*

While she considered her impending trip to town, Myra took light bread from the cupboard, American cheese slices from the refrigerator, and a can of sardines from the pantry. She hardly looked as she snapped the key from the sardine can and rolled back the top; nor as she put her sandwich together with an experienced hand. She scarcely tasted as she ate, standing at the kitchen sink. She washed down her hurried lunch with a jelly glassful of tap water, rinsed the glass and up-ended it on the counter. She was a woman with a mission that had nothing to do with her own nourishment.

She would go straight to the stores, she'd decided, make her necessary purchases, and be back before school turned out. Grocery buying could wait till the boys could go with her.

For the first time in her life, Myra wished she had a telephone. She wanted to hear from Sandy and Wiley, and she wanted to know about Merrill's funeral. Another thing, she ought to buy some flowers for her dead father-in-law.

Driving back from the stores, Myra felt as if she had bought exactly what Sandy would like in her and her new husband's bedroom. That was the prettiest shade of pink that Myra had ever seen, and it looked kind of silky. Sandy hadn't had much in her life–Myra could surely tell that; and some pretty pink sheets and things would be good for her.

She saw Vonceil walking toward her house, and she stopped. "You goin' down to see me?" she inquired.

"Well, I was—shore was. I didn't know you was gone."

"Ain't gone no more," laughed Myra. "Git in, an' we'll both go to my house."

Vonceil clambered into the pickup. She had noticed a big packing crate in the truck bed and when she saw the packages in the cab, her need to know things was almost overwhelming.

"You been a-shoppin'?"

"Yeah, I shore have. My, uh, my sister an' her husband's comin' in sometime today an' I was just gittin' their bedroom fixed up for 'em."

"Oh, your sister? Is that th' pregnant girl I seen up there Saturday?"

"Anh-hanh. They been off on a little trip an' they're comin' back in today."

"Who did you tell me she was married to?"

"He's a preacher–name of Wiley Spells. You musta saw him Saturday, too, a-drivin' that there movin' truck."

Vonceil was really put out with herself. She had been so sure that something was shady down there on the end of Paglan Street, but now come to find out that pretty girl's really married–and married to a preacher, at that.

"Tell you what, Miz Boone, I better just git out an' go on back to th' house. I plumb forgot to feed them chickens, an' you know you ain't gonna git no eggs outta no hungry chickens. I 'preciate th' ride, though. Y'all come to see me soon as you can."

Then, "When they gonna bury Merrill?"

"I dunno right now, Miz Haggerty, but when I find out, I'll letcha know."

## HONEYMOONERS, COME HOME

When Roy and Barney came from school, Myra put them to work at once. "Go git that big ol' carton outta th' pickup, an' hurry, now, 'cause we got to git it set up before they git here."

The "big ol' carton" contained a pink baby bed. "I don't know why in th' world we didn't think to git th' baby somethin' to sleep in," she told the boys. "I reckon we was so bent on gittin' grown-folks furniture, we never even thought about it."

Before their work had been finished more than a few minutes, Sandy and Wiley drove up. Myra and Roy and Barney raced out to meet them as if they'd been gone a year. There was much hugging and laughing, much inviting into the house and carrying in of paper sacks.

"Sandy, I can't wait for y'all to see your bedroom. We got it all fixed so pretty for you. I was really movin' around this mornin', tryin' to git it all done before y'all got here."

"Oh, Myra, you done so good. How you reckon I'm ever gonna thank you for makin' it so pretty, an' for gettin' th' baby's little bed? Oh, Myra! Oh, look, Wiley, darlin', how pretty it all is!"

Wiley agreed with great enthusiasm that this was the prettiest room he'd ever seen. He patted Myra, exclaiming, "If there ever was a friend, Myra, you're at th' top of th' list. I just hope we can repay you some day for all the good things you've done."

They soon made their way to the front porch and the familiar comfort of the rocking chairs, where the talk turned to Merrill's funeral, and to Naomi out there with only the servants. The mourners had gone about first light, Sandy told Myra, and the place was quiet. Wheeler was not to be found there, and nobody seemed to know where he had gone.

"Myra, Naomi told me to mention to you that they are bringing Hayden to th' funeral."

Sandy had kept a watchful eye on Myra as she delivered the news, caught Myra's quick intake of breath and saw her gladness before she could get her face straight. Myra brought her rocking chair to a sudden halt. Then, realizing how inappropriate her response might seem, she changed the subject.

"When is th' funeral, Sandy? I reckon Naomi's decided by now."

"It's gonna be tomorrow, right there at th' workshop. Four o'clock. An' they're planning to bury him in that plot there back of th' house. Naomi wants to keep him pretty close."

After supper they all sat on the porch again. Wiley and Sandy did most of the talking while Myra chimed in on a rather subdued note from time to time. She was thinking about seeing Hayden again, and wondering what he would say about the events that had changed all their lives in these past few days. She hoped he would like Sandy, and that he would be supportive of her moving to town.

Then she worried, *what if they was to bring him to th' funeral in chains or somethin'?*

She heard Sandy call her name. "Hey, there, girl. You ain't even listenin', are you?"

"Hanh? I think I was about to fall asleep. Did I miss somethin'?"

"Naw. I was just sayin' that Wiley's going on out to Naomi's first thing in th' morning, an' I thought I'd stay here with you an' go out there when you an' th' young'uns go. Is that all right?"

"Oh, yeah, Sandy — do that. Me an' you ain't had no chance to talk in I don't know when."

They all laughed, and Wiley said, "Great day! It's been a whole twenty-four hours since you girls talked!" Then,

"What is it y'all say to one another all th' time? Are y'all plottin' against me already?"

Sandy squeezed his hand and whispered, "Lord, how did I get so happy?"

## VONCEIL/JIM DANDY TO THE RESCUE

After Wiley left the next morning, Sandy and Myra sat down at the kitchen table with a second cup of coffee. Although nobody had mentioned Wheeler the night before, both women kept returning to the dread of what he might do to destroy their paradise.

"Myra, what we gonna do about 'im? You know he ain't gonna just let it go."

She had hardly finished saying it when Myra, suddenly alert, said, "Shh! That's that ol' Peterbilt tractor comin' down th' street."

She ran to the front door, latched the screen and bolted the wood door just as Wheeler pulled up before the house. By way of announcing his arrival, he blew three long blasts of the tractor's air horn. It was enough to get the neighbors' attention.

Letting the engine run, Wheeler stepped out and onto the yard. From the window, Myra could see him very clearly, and she could tell he was drunk. Again or still, she didn't speculate.

"Myra!" he hollered. "Myra Boone, you worthless bitch, come ou'chere! Whur's that whorin' buddy'a yorn? Bring her ou'chere, too. I got some goddam news t'tell you sluts!"

Vonceil Haggerty heard him. She ran to her telephone and rang the sheriff's office.

"Sheriff Royster? This is Vonceil Haggerty, over on Paglan Street–they's a crazy fool over here a-raisin' hell like you ain't never heard tell of. Can you send somebody to put his sorry ass in jail before I hav'ta take my gun an' go kill 'im?–He's a-drivin' a bobtail, an' he's down at Miz Boone's house.–Well, you come on, Sher'ff, but I'm gonna beat you there!"

She rang off and dashed out of her house, running down the street toward the Boone's place. When she had gone more than half way, she paused to listen some more to Wheeler's raving before she picked up the pace again.

When she was within what she considered striking distance, and still running, she yelled, "Sher'ff Royster's on his way down here, mister. An' if you want t'know, I'm th' one that called 'im. This here's a good, family neighborhood, an' we gonna keep it like that if we havta put you under th' jail! You hear me, sir? You got just about two shakes to git back in your little bobtail an' haul it outta here!

Wheeler, despite his drunken condition, recognized the implacable voice of authority when he heard it. He figured he had too much to do to waste a day in jail. *Mama don't know from a rat's ass how to run that damn farm,* he told himself. *She'll jes' let them damn niggers drag they sorry butts around an' lay out an' not git a goddam thaing did. She'd be a helluva sight better off a-thankin' God she kin depend on me, instead 'a gittin' so goddam worked up over that slut, Myra, an' that bitchin' Sandy.*

He drew himself up, whirled and climbed back aboard his tractor. He would be back–they could all count on it. For one small instant, he considered running down that old heifer that had hollered at him, but he changed his mind and whipped on by her, cursing her as he went.

Myra and Sandy rushed out to thank Vonceil, but she waved away their gratitude with, "I live here, too, y'know, an' I ain't havin' no sich doin's goin' on where I live." She turned back toward her house with, "Y'all come to see me when you git around to it."

As they turned back toward the porch, Sandy paused, suppressing a gasp. Myra caught her arm, and turned to face her.

"Sandy, do you know for shore when th' baby's comin'? I notice you movin' mighty slow. What did your doctor tell you about a due date?"

"Aw, Myra. You know I ain't been to no doctor. I reckon it's pretty plain I'm pregnant, an' I been feelin' all right. Ain't no need for no doctor till it's time."

"Well, go on in yonder an' see if you can lay down some before we have to go t'Naomi's. An' lemme see about the young'uns–see if they a-hidin' under th' bed from Wheeler."

## LET YOUR TEARDROPS KISS TH'
## FLOWERS ON MY GRAVE

It looked as if everybody in six counties had come for Merrill's funeral. Cars were parked clear back to the highway, and sheriff's deputies were directing traffic. As soon as they saw Myra's pickup, they waved her through.

"They savin' some space up yonder for you, Miz Boone," Deputy Grassley told her.

The space they'd saved was right up close to the workshop, and Sandy was grateful she wouldn't have far to walk. She wasn't feeling as well as she'd made out like. Mostly tired, she decided, but when this was over, she meant to go back to the house and get in bed.

In the meantime, Sandy tried to focus her attention on Myra and her dark blue dress, her low-heeled pumps and the wry comments she'd made about wearing her own funeral clothes to somebody else's funeral. *All in all*, thought Sandy, *Myra looks real nice.*

When they walked into the building, Hayden was the first person Myra saw. He was standing down front, talking to a man in a dark blue suit. She didn't know it was the prison guard, sent to make sure he went back to Reidsville.

"Y'all set down wherever you want to," Myra said to her companions, "I'm goin' to speak to Hayden."

He had seen her, too, and he started back up the aisle to meet her. They met about half way and there was never a doubt of the need for them to embrace each other. Both of them held on for a long moment.

"I hoped so hard you'd come," she whispered.

"I knew I had to," he told her. "I just wish we could talk before I go back." He looked into her face. "Myra–Myra, honey, I wish I didn't never have to–I mean, are you all right?"

The pallbearers were gathering near the door, and Myra turned to find her seat with Sandy and the boys. Hayden went back to the blue-suited stranger.

Naomi remembered Merrill joking about long funerals in other days. "When I go, just get Willie an' them to dig me a grave out yonder back of th' house, an' put me down. Don't have no big to-do about it."

But here she was, having a big to-do. Two preachers had to go on about what a good man he was–something everybody already knew; and a third one felt compelled to recite all the honors that had been bestowed upon a man who lost his leg in an heroic rescue in World War II. Naomi hoped Merrill wasn't blaming her for all this carrying on.

She wondered fleetingly where Wheeler was. Since she'd turned Wheeler over to God, he didn't trouble her much. Knowing God had His eye on Wheeler was good enough for Naomi. Her duty lay in following God's directions about what He wanted her to do now.

Wheeler came, after all. Just before the benediction, he strode into the chapel and down the aisle to the front. It was obvious to the congregation that Wheeler was a man possessed by drink.

"Who told y'all you could have a damn funeral ou'chere on my damn propitty an' not eb'n ast my perdamnmission?

Did my damn jailbird brother say it was okay? Well, he ain't got no hell-fired say-so..."

Sheriff Royster, sitting there with the other pallbearers, was directly behind his chief deputy, Lonnie Ray O'Steen. He touched Lonnie Ray on the shoulder, and the two men rose silently. Without a word, they approached Wheeler, right and left, and caught him just under each arm, lifting him off the floor. They turned him around and walked him out of the chapel while the third preacher pronounced God's blessing on the mourners.

Deputy O'Steen drove back to Harlow with a handcuffed Wheeler slumped over in the back seat of the cruiser, passed out. At the jail, two more deputies carried him in and laid him on a cot in a cell.

"Let's charge 'im with disturbin' th' peace," suggested Deputy O'Steen, "since we ain't got no law against bein' a straight-out fool."

*HOME, WHERE THE HEART IS*

Naomi, for all her demonstrated strength, began to wane after the funeral. With her newly-configured family group and a few long-time friends, she walked back to the house and they all took seats on the commodious front porch. Arlena and Mary brought light refreshments, passing silver trays laden with delicate, white-meat chicken sandwiches, shaved-ham morsels on beaten biscuits, sour cream pound cake, chocolate-rum almond cookies, chilled white grapes, melon balls and strong, black coffee. The conversation centered on the safest sort of uplifting subject matter. They spoke in gentle reverence of the splendid day God had appointed for Merrill's home going, of the beauty of the Boone's plantation, of the hospitality all of them had enjoyed over the years at the hands of their hostess and her late husband.

"Do y'all remember that night Hayden fell off th' end of th' porch when he was a-hidin', a-tryin' to hear what th' grown folks was sayin'? An' all the time, Naomi thought that young'un was in bed, asleep?" Archie Vandiver had not forgotten it. He told about it again, as he did every time he came to the Boone's house. It was a story that never failed to bring indulgent laughter. And every time he told it, Mollie Warner would say, as she did that day, "I cain't eb'n recollect what we was a-talkin' about, but hit musta been somethin' racy." True to tradition, that, too, got a laugh.

After that, talk turned to likely prospects for a hot summer and a re-telling of the effects of last year's "coldest Georgia winter on record" and the possibilities for that year's bumper crop of cotton.

Wheeler's participation in the funeral was never mentioned on the porch, but Arlena and Mary went over it with Willie and his sons back in the kitchen.

"He gonna keep on till somebody have to kill 'im," predicted Arlena. "An' today I was wishin' it'd be me that would get to do it."

Willie's distress took another direction. "You reckon he think he gonna run us off? This ain't th' first time he been cussin' us an' callin' us 'damn niggers,' like he was doin' las' night."

On the porch, Myra kept an eye on Sandy, who quietly rocked, smiling from time to time at her new husband. *Somethin' about her don't look right,* thought Myra. *I got to git her to a doctor tomorrow.*

The sun was setting when Myra and Roy and Barney got up to leave. Myra had declined the invitation to stay for supper, feeling an urgent need to go back to their house on Paglan Street. She urged Sandy and Wiley to come with them, and Sandy stood up, apparently glad of the chance to go back home.

Once they got to the house, everybody began to know some relief from the stressful events of the past few days. They had all done their duty in every way they knew how, and it was time for a rest. Supper was easy and relaxed, and even Roy and Barney ventured into the conversation once in awhile.

"Lord, we've all been through th' mill, ain't we?" exclaimed Myra. "I bet ain't nobody on th' place gonna be to rock to sleep tonight."

Wiley herded the women out to the porch after the meal, declaring that he and the boys would clean up the kitchen.

"You ladies do too much all th' time," he said, "an' I'm gonna try to stop some of that. Me an' Roy an' Barney can do chores here, too, you know. So go on, now — kick back a little." He kissed his bride. "Rest some, darlin', please. For you an' our baby, if not for nobody else."

Dragging her chair closer to Sandy, Myra smiled at the new bride.

"Sometime, things goes so right that it's plumb scary, ain't it?"

## YESSIR, THAT'S MY BABY

The two women had been on the porch but a short time when Sandy suddenly cried, "Myra! MYRA! It's the baby! I got to get to th' hospital. Oh, God, Myra! I'm hurtin' so bad!"

On her feet, Myra screamed for Wiley.

"Come out here, Wiley! Quick!"

Wiley, followed by Roy and Barney, ran to the porch. Wiley was at Sandy's side, trying to take hold of her.

"Darlin', don't cry. We're goin' right now! Come on, sweetheart, hold on to me!"

Myra swung around, ordering, "Git th' truck keys, Roy, an' y'all come on."

Roy dashed back for the keys while Wiley and Myra got Sandy into Wiley's car. She was moaning, crying out, scared and in pain. As soon as they could close the car door, Wiley ran to the other side and got in.

"Y'all come on quick as you can," he told Myra, pulling away. The boys ran to Myra, Roy holding the pickup keys.

"We got 'em, Mama. Let's go!" The three of them raced to the pickup, clambered in and careened out of the yard, wheels spinning, a thick cloud of dust, leaves and twigs rising in their wake.

At the hospital, emergency room personnel recognized Wiley, their new chaplain, and sent orderlies running to his car with a guerney for Sandy. By then, she was writhing, screaming at top volume, wild tears racing down her cheeks in a salty flood.

"Call Dr. Marshall," snapped Terri Hendricks, the charge nurse, to her assistant. "Tell 'im we got us a baby on th' way. Right now!"

Wiley, wild-eyed and distraught, was taken quickly to a waiting area. His nurse-escort was brisk.

"You just sit down right here, Reverend. We'll keep you posted, but we don't need you in yonder 'cause we gonna be busy."

Myra and the boys hurried in at the front of the building and were directed to the maternity waiting room where they found a weeping Wiley on his knees in prayer. Myra knelt down beside him and put her arm across his shoulder.

"She's gonna be all right, Wiley. She's just havin' a baby, Wiley—it happens all th' time."

Three endless hours later, Dr. Marshall came to them. His countenance was, well, kind of strange. Myra caught it first. *My God*, she thought, *Sandy's bad off—oh, Lord...*

"You've got a beautiful little girl, Reverend Spells. She's just perfect."

Wiley reached both hands to the doctor, as if to embrace him, or perhaps as a gesture of supplication.

"Sandy. How 'bout Sandy? Is Sandy gonna be all right, doctor?"

Myra's fears took shape then. Dr. Marshall stumbled as he tried to explain.

"Well, ah, Reverend, Mrs. Spells has, ah, had a hard time here tonight. I don't know if she's mentioned it, but she's apparently been having some trouble with this pregnancy. Another thing, her general health wasn't really the best for getting pregnant..."

"Talk to me, doctor! I wanta know about my wife! How is my wife?"

"Ah, Mr. Spells, ah, I want you to sit down here and let's talk about what we're up against. I know you're a man of God, and you have to get a grip on yourself. You know, God watches over us all, all the time—you ought to know that better than anybody. Now, Mrs. Spells is not in good shape. We're doing everything we can do for her—every doctor in the State of Georgia couldn't do more than we're doing. But it's not looking good right now. Let's just wait a little bit and see how things go. I'm going to let you all go in to see her in a minute, but you've got to pull yourselves together. You can't let her see you like this."

Wiley had slumped back in his chair, pain contorting his face, tears gushing from his eyes. Myra continued to stand there, stunned. Color had drained from her face. *So this is how God treats pore little ol' girls when they git th' first good chance they ever had. It ain't fair a-tall. Not a damn thing fair about it. Naomi. That's who can deal with this situation.*

Myra turned away in search of a telephone. *Naomi will know what to do; what to say to this God that don't care no more'n this for one 'a His very own that's already had such a hard time.*

*Sandy ain't never hurt nobody! Naomi's got a right damn lots of explainin' to do, too, since she's th' one always talkin' Him up.*

Presently, Wiley and Myra were taken to Sandy's room. She looked pale, tired, used up, but she smiled when she saw them. Wiley clasped her to his bosom and murmured words of endearment while Myra fought her tears and smiled at Sandy.

"They're gonna bring our baby in here in a minute for y'all to see," said Sandy. "That's th' prettiest little baby girl in th' whole world. Oh, Lord, she's just as pretty as a pitchur. Got a whole bunch 'a red hair. Just wait—you gonna see how pretty she is."

"She better be pretty, or she ain't yores," teased Myra.

When Nurse Hendricks brought the newborn, she eased her down into Sandy's arms. Even Myra's guard came down. The baby was, indeed, a beauty.

Despite her own tears of joy, Sandy's smile was bright as she told Wiley, "Look, darlin', it's our own little baby girl."

Wiley tenderly touched the baby's hair, answering, "Yes, my love, our own little girl—yours and mine."

Myra watched the nurse's face, her apprehension growing. Nurse Hendricks' mouth was smiling, but something about her eyes looked grave. She seemed anxious to take the baby back to the nursery.

I'll try to bring her back soon," she told Sandy, lifting the baby from its mother's arms. "You rest, now. If you need me..."

Holding Wiley's hand in both of hers, Sandy made the announcement that was most important to her.

"I know what I'm wantin' to name her, if it's all right with you, Wiley, darlin'."

Sandy could do no wrong in Wiley's eyes. "Anything you want to name her is fine with me. Tell us what's your pleasure."

"Y'all are th' dearest things in th' world to me, Wiley, you an' Myra. Ain't nobody in my life ever loved me like y'all do, an' you don't never ask for nothin' in return. So, I want to name this here baby girl, 'Wildwood Myra Spells.' Every time anybody calls her name, they gonna know that I loved th' two of y'all with every bit of strength I had."

She turned her smile on Myra and added, "I really want her to take after you–you're my hero." Turning back to Wiley, Sandy took one last, longing look at her beloved before she closed her green eyes on this world forever.

It was over. Myra left a wailing Wiley there, holding the lifeless body of his beautiful wife, and walked back out to her boys. Her grief would go with her for the rest of her life.

# 7

# "If A Man Not Repent—"

*LIFE GOES ON SOMEHOW*
Carmen Kirby from the Beauty Patch had come to the funeral home to style Sandy's hair and put her make-up on. Gaston's never let a female body go on display until Carmen had worked her magic. This time, Carmen lingered to help dress the body, admiring of the shroud the family had chosen. To herself she concluded, *Them folks got style.*

Myra and Naomi had come to view Carmen's handiwork before the body was arranged in the coffin. Until they set eyes upon the readied corpse, Myra had forgotten that she and Sandy had something to hide from Naomi. A startled Myra watched as Naomi laid a gentle hand on Sandy's shapely little foot and uttered the gracious, forgiving words, "Them's right pretty little toe nails, ain't they?"

Sandy's funeral was a lot smaller than Merrill's, but the level of grief was comparable. Wiley and Myra, Roy and Barney wept uncontrollably. Willie and Arlena and Mary and Raiford and Toby hovered in the second pew and mourned for Sandy, for her inconsolable husband and for her bereft–though lately acquired–family. Naomi sat in regal, stunned silence, wondering if God had momentarily looked off.

Dr. Marshall had come, as had Sheriff Royster; Dwight Monk's secretary, Pearl Hadsock, at her boss's direction, was present. He had told her by long distance telephone the night before what Naomi Boone had wanted with him, and she attended in Dwight's absence–standing in for him, you might say. She almost wished he hadn't told her; not knowing, she might not have cried so much.

Vonceil Haggerty had arrived early, accompanied by a short, stout, older man who hobbled with a metal crutch. Throughout the service, he just sat and stared straight ahead, reaching a time or two to pat his weeping wife. Once, she said aloud, "She shore was pretty." Her observation intensified the wailing.

There on the premises, in the Boone family plot, they lowered Sandy's body–resplendently clad in Myra's flowered chiffon wedding dress and her brassy little sandals–into a newly-dug grave right close to Merrill's. It was the space Naomi had earlier planned for Wheeler's remains.

When it was done, Wiley and Myra and her children drove back to town in Wiley's car. By prearrangement, they stopped by the hospital to pick up Wildwood Myra Spells, two days old, and take her home.

*I GUESS I BEEN WAITIN' FOR YOU*

By midnight, everybody at the Paglan Street house was asleep except for Myra Boone. She walked the hall in her bare feet–back to the kitchen, through the dining room, through the living room, out to the hall. She looked out the glass panel on the front door time and again.

Now what? She planned to ask Wiley–beg him, if that's what it took–to stay here, him and the baby, with her and the boys. She was strong, and she could handle the care of the baby. She thought back to the night she told Sandy she would raise the child because it was Wheeler's. *No more of that,* she thought. *I'll raise it now because it's Sandy's. An' Wheeler, well, he can just go to hell.*

Whatever she used to feel for Wheeler was gone, and all she wanted from him now was his absence. Later on, when the baby was old enough, Myra could get a job there in Harlow. Right now, her money in the carpetbag was holding out pretty good. They had just about everything they needed for a good while.

She was not surprised when she heard the Peterbilt bobtail turn down Paglan Street. She really had been expecting it. She stood beside the front door, patiently awaiting Wheeler's arrival.

She heard him shut down the "mons-ster," as Sandy had called it, heard him slam the door as he got down. And she heard his opening bellow, "MYRA! You sorry slut! Git yore ass ou'chere, you whore! I got somethin' to say t'you!—You hear me, you goddam crazy heifer?"

Silence.

"MYRA! You hear me, you bitch? I'm comin' in there! All them damn young'uns you so goddam crazy about is MINE! By God, they ever' damn one of em's MINE!

Wiley was beside Myra. He whispered, "I thought he was in jail."

"They let him out on bond, just like they do drunks like that. I'd call somebody, but Lord, we ain't got no way to call."

Wheeler's hollering did not abate. He finally played his trump card.

"MYRA! I'm fixin' t'come in there an' I'm gonna kill ever' sonuvabitch on th' place! You better say yore goddam prayers, you damn uncivilized Injun slut, 'cause you fixin' t'die! All of you are a-fixin' t'die."

Myra and Wiley watched in horror as Wheeler opened the tractor door and brought out the deer rifle, the one with the scope.

"He got in th' house an' got that thing when we was at church Sunday," lamented Myra. "An' eb'n drunk, he can bring down a deer plumb acrost th' county."

Wheeler swung the weapon upward, expertly fitting the butt against his shoulder, making ready to fire.

Myra nodded, as if she'd made a decision. "That's all right, Mr. Wheeler Boone. You done made yore last threat on this family."

The revolver was in her hand, drawn from the back waistband of her jeans. Wiley's eyes widened. "Myra! What're you doin'?"

"I'm fixin' t' kill that there sonuvabitch," she whispered.

She opened the door, raised the gun and fired. Just once.

Wiley's frantic cries of, "NO, MYRA! NO!" were lost in the report that echoed and echoed and echoed through the still of the night.

"Myra, you goddam bit–" He fell. Wheeler Boone, hard-working, truck-driving, family man, fell and died there in the dust at the end of Paglan Street without ever saying all he'd come to say. Or doing all he'd come to do.

*LAW & ORDER*

Naomi was in the car with Sheriff Royster when he rolled down Paglan Street that morning just after nine o'clock. When he picked her up at the Boone plantation half an hour earlier, his opening comments were mild enough.

"I would have come got you sooner, Naomi, but we had us a bad night—a couple of wrecks we had to work. Wasn't nobody bad hurt, but they takened time. An' I was a-needin' to do some more investigatin' before I could get with you. I went on an' got me some statements an' made me some phone calls, but just like I figured all the time, this here Wheeler thing wasn't nothin' but self defense, open an' shut. Ain't no doubts about that."

"I know you're right, Sheriff. Myra wouldn't do nothin' like that unless she had it to do. Myra, she never has been th' violent kind."

"But back to what I was sayin'. I called that there truckin' company that Wheeler works for last night an' talked to th' little lady that was on duty. She was mighty upset over Wheeler bein' dead; said he was engaged to her cousin over in Macclenny. Been goin' with her for two or three months, she told me. She even said he was gonna make out his insurance to her, but he never did get around to it. I'm right sorry to have to say it, Naomi, but it looks like Wheeler had a mean eye for a low fence."

Naomi didn't argue the point.

"An' when O'Steen went through his tractor, he found one of them little bank books in a zipped-up, inside pocket of his leather jacket. That scaper's got a whole bunch of money in a bank in Jacksonsville—been saltin' cash away for more than ten years. It's done run up to near 'bout $35,000. Reckon how come he was doin' that?"

Naomi stared down at her hands clenched in her lap. For years, she had rejected the suspicion that Wheeler was a man without integrity; a secretive, deceitful man who used everybody.

"I don't know, Sheriff. I just don't know."

"I did find out, though," Royster went on, "that he really did have a big insurance policy on hisself. Truckin' company seen to that. That woman told me it'd probably run to a hundred thousand dollars or more, an' it's still made out to Myra."

They rode in silence for awhile, and he added,

"I told that there woman she could tell her cousin she might be just as well off with Wheeler Boone out of th' picture."

Then, "I tell you somethin' else, Naomi, I come in a inch of tellin' th' coroner to put Wheeler's death down to suicide, an' I would've did it if it hadn't been for that there insurance. He was just plain askin' for it."

He reached under the seat and brought out a big brown envelope, which he passed over to Naomi.

"Here's thirty-eight one-hundred-dollar bills. Four of them, an' a couple of tens, was in his pocket, an' th' rest of them was hid up under th' seat of his tractor—had them fastened up under there with ol' duct tape. Look like he was a-holdin' out on Myra ever'whichaway."

Naomi reached across the seat and patted Royster's arm.

"Sheriff, you somethin' else. You know that?"

When they reached their destination, Naomi stepped up onto the porch ahead of the sheriff and went inside.

"Myra? Y'all all right? Is th' baby all right?"

Wiley came from the kitchen to meet her, holding the tiny, red-haired baby, giving her a bottle. "Come on in, Naomi; you're the answer to a prayer. Myra's out on th' back porch with Roy an' Barney. They're just sittin' out there. Waitin' on th' sheriff, I reckon. I wish you'd go on out there an' see if you can talk to her."

Naomi kept on through the house and to the back porch. Myra was sitting on the top step, Roy and Barney huddled against each other on the next step down. The three of them were holding hands, and nobody saying a word.

"Myra? Come on in an' let's drink some coffee. I bet Roy an' Barney's a-wantin' some hot chocolate. Come on in, now."

Sheriff Royster appeared in the hall. "She out there?"

"Anh-hanh," Naomi told him. "I'll get her in here in a minute. Go on in th' kitchen, Sheriff–pour yourself a cup of coffee."

Myra stood, pulling the boys up with her, and turned to the door. "Might as well go on in, boys. Naomi's here."

Myra saw Sheriff Royster as she turned into the kitchen. "I been expectin' you," she greeted him.

"Miz Boone, this here's just routine. I'm gonna have to say I interviewed you, but I done got me some statements from th' reverend, there, an' from Vonceil, up yonder. It don't look like much will come of this here episode. Why don't you just sit down right here, an' let's get this thing over with?"

Myra sat, looking up at the sheriff. "I reckon I meant to do it, Sheriff," she said, "but I'm always gonna be sorry I had to take his life. I know it's too late to be makin' apologies about it, though, 'cause he's dead. I just hate I had to kill them three young'uns's daddy. Maybe, if I could've..."

Myra turned her tear-stained face away, but not before he saw the evident pain and remorse. He hated that; Wheeler Boone would not be terribly missed in Harlow, Georgia, and certainly not by anybody in the sheriff's office.

"Now, Miz Boone. Now, he was out there a-threatenin' all of y'all, wasn't he? Sayin' he was gonna come in here an' kill all of you? Th' neighbors heard all that, Miz Boone. They done told me they heard it. An' Miz Haggerty up yonder, she's th' one that called my office th' other day when he was down here a-raisin' hell. That's on my log at th' office, time of day an' everything. It's on th' record, him a-cuttin' th' fool. An' remember, I was out yonder at Merrill's funeral when he showed his butt an' we had to take him out an' put him in jail.

"Lord knows, we kept him up there as long as we could, but we just didn't have enough on him to keep holdin' him. An' we didn't know he had that there rifle, like he did. Miz Boone, I feel kindly responsible, myself, for what's takened place here, an' I don't see no reason to do nothin' to you about it. If it's all right with you, I'm just gonna go ahead an' write up my report an' say on there that this here shootin' was straight-out self defense, an' let it go at that. Is they somethin' else you was a-wantin' me to do?"

Myra slid her coffee spoon to the edge of the table and back again toward the cup. All she could see were the flowers on the oilcloth and that silver-colored spoon sliding along the slick surface. *That there spoon's pretty,* she thought; *I wished we'd 'a got us a whole set of 'em. Maybe they still got some left at th' store...*

At last, she returned to a realization of where she was and what was happening: Sheriff Royster was still standing there, looking down at her. *I know I ought to say somethin',* she thought, *or do somethin'. This man could've put handcuffs on me an' put me in jail, an' here I am just settin' here, not even thankin' him, nor nothin'.*

She got to her feet, reaching a hand to the sheriff. "I shore 'preciate what you're a-doin', Sheriff. If you was to change yore mind an' decide you was a-needin' me to go to jail, you just come on back an' git me."

"Not no chance of that, Miz Boone. This here case is closed."

He took her proffered hand and, when he shook it, he noticed how rough it was. He'd shaken many a hand in his lifetime, and he knew what made a hand rough like Myra Boone's–nothing but hard work for a long, long time. She hadn't had much of a life.

Sheriff Royster stood there for a moment, looking at Myra, taking in her faded shirt, her washed-out jeans, her worn moccasins. Her eyes were swollen from crying, her hair in disarray. He wished he knew some way to comfort her.

He reached across the oil cloth and gave her bony shoulder an awkward pat.

"Any time you think you need somethin' from my office, Miz Boone, you be shore an' call us."

"I shore thank you, Sheriff. I'm gonna git us a phone put in here today just so we can call you if we was to ever feel th' need."

Myra sank back into her chair, suddenly stricken with the memory of the last time she'd needed to call the law. Sheriff Royster read her expression, sensing that she was re-living the night before.

"Well, all right." He stood there in an uneasy silence. At last, "Well, let us hear from you, Miz Boone." He turned on his heel and moved back into the hall.

*Hell,* he thought, as he strode back to his cruiser, *some things is just mor'n a mortal man can handle.*

### WISH YOU WAS HERE, SANDY

"Sheriff, you go on back, an' I'll get me a ride home after while. I think I'll stay here with th' baby an' them for a little bit an' get acquainted with my granddaughter."

It was Naomi. She'd known in advance what the sheriff meant to say to Myra, so she had no further need to climb into a sheriff's cruiser. *Them things makes me nervous,* she thought, glad to escape another ride with the law.

Naomi went back in the kitchen to find Myra sitting again at the table, playing with the spoon.

"Myra," she began, "Dwight Monk called me just before I left th' house this mornin' — he just got back from Atlanta late last night. He was up there to see th' governor an' th' pardon board."

Myra looked up. *What was Naomi talkin' about?*

"He did?"

"Anh-hanh. Merrill talked to Dwight about it a good while back, an' he's been a-workin' on it. He finally got it arranged yesterday. Looks like Hayden's gonna be out of Reidsville in th' next day or two. They got to fix th' paperwork an' all. I thought you'd want to know. An' you know what? He had to get that trooper to go all th' way to Atlanta to get him to tell th' governor what really happened — that he drawed on Hayden first. He claimed he thought Hayden was somebody else when he first stopped him. Said he took that boy for a dang fugitive they'd been a-lookin' for. Dwight says they all had a good laugh over that.

Myra didn't move for a long time, just sat there with her mouth slightly open. Naomi watched.

*Well, now,* she thought. *Did I miss somethin'? Come to think of it, Myra's th' one that's kept on a-visitin' Hayden in Reidsville, an' seem like I wondered a little bit about th' two of them at Merrill's funeral. I just told her he's gettin' out because I thought she'd be glad we're a-gettin' what's left of th' family back together.*

When Myra's eyes met Naomi's, tears were starting. She dragged the back of her hand across her eyes the way a child might do, and offered Naomi a crumpled smile.

"I wish Sandy could've knowed that before she left."

Across the centuries, Ruth's word echoed in Naomi's heart –"...the Lord do so to me, and more also, if ought but death part thee and me"–and she touched her daughter-in-law's cheek with great tenderness.

"I expect she does, Myra, I expect she does. Her an' Merrill both."

"You reckon?"

"Yeah, I reckon. In th' wind-up, God don't never let us down."